The
Red
Menace

a fiction

michael anania

Thunder's Mouth Press   New York • Chicago

Published in the United States by Thunder's Mouth
Press, Box 780, New York NY 10025 and Box 11223,
Chicago, IL 60611
Design by Randee Berman
Cover photo by Dale Debolt
Grateful acknowledgment is made to the New York State
Council on the Arts and the National Endowment for the
Arts for financial assistance with the publication of this
volume.
The chapters titled "The Red Menace" and "Autoclysms"
first appeared in Tri-Quarterly. *"I do not know this sad-*
ness . . ." and "The Death of Mrs. Rich" first appeared in
Chicago.
This book was completed with the help of a fellowship
from the Illinois Arts Council.

Annie Had a Baby, copyright 1954
Words and Music by Henry Glover and Lois Mann

Let the Good Times Roll, copyright 1956
Words and Music by Leonard Lee

Library of Congress Cataloging in Publication Data
Anania, Michael, 1939–
    The red menace.

    I. Title.
PS3551.N25R4   1984   813'.54   83-24171
ISBN 0-938410-19-1

Distributed by
Persea Books
225 Lafayette St.
New York NY 10012
(212) 431-5270

for David Bahr,
              who was there
and Elliott Anderson,
              who was not

good morning to you, we're all in our places

A frayed army blanket trailed off the daybed toward the kitchen. Blue-gray television light bounced over the walls to the movements of the chimpanzee dancing on the screen—J. Fred Muggs conducting the morning. A small light from outside edged the ice that leaned in half-stalagmites on the iron-framed living room windows. There were two cushioned chairs facing the television and a wire telephone stand next to the kitchen archway, one of those imitation brass occasional pieces shown in dime store windows with optional electric blue or salmon pink fitted ashtray for the top and a matching flowerpot in a brass ring at one side. It was the same living room they all had. The mixture of hand-me-down furniture and Woolworth's gaiety varied only slightly from apartment to apartment. A boy seated on the edge of the daybed pulled off his stocking cap and brushed away the beads of water the snow had left on his hair. In the chair nearest the window another boy was opening his peacoat. Richard came to the kitchen door in socks, shorts, and an unbuttoned plaid flannel shirt, scraping at the bottom of a carton of cottage cheese with a soup spoon. His Levi's were warming on the kitchen radiator. It was his hedge against the cold, waiting to slip them on until the last moment.

"It's at six-thirty."
"Where's Reuben?"
"Don't ask me."
"Can you fix that thing?"
"Man, soon as you get your own television, you can start complainin' 'bout mine."
"I ain't complainin', Richard."
"Sure do sound like it to me."
"Me too."
"You shut up, else I'll pop you upside your head."

There were puppets on the screen, black bushmen puppets with black, woolly, hair that jerked wildly, as the puppets danced in front of a grass hut. The record they shook to was "Dance With Me Henry," a hit parade version of "Annie Had a Baby," a black song with a tense, anti-social presence about it.

Annie had a baby,
Cain't work no more!
Annie had a baby,
Cain't work no more!

Richard sang his way back into the kitchen, and Gerald and Herman growled the bass. "Uh, u-uh, uh, u-uh."

You thought it would happen,
You knew that it could,
But that's what happens
When the gittin' gits good!
Whooooooo.

"Man, don't that puppet remind you a Ruby?"

Herman was half out of his chair. "I'll kick your weasel ass," then more in keeping with the game, "I didn't know your mama's name was Ruby."

"It ain't."

8

There was a clamor at the door—Reuben in a sheepskin flier's jacket, brown hide flaking at all the creases like scabs, his head and shoulders covered with snow, pompadour frozen into a black iceberg. "Colder than a well-digger's ass in Alaska." He unwound his white rayon scarf. "Colder than an Eskimo well-digger's ass." He stamped his engineer boots on the concrete floor. "Colder than a snowman's balls."

"Will you shut up, man."

"Colder than an ice-house whore."

"Shut up, man, it's gonna start."

"What the fuck's an ice-house whore?"

"Your mama. Now, shut up, man, it's starting."

"Your mama."

The puppets were gone, and the screen showed a gray, flat space, a single wooden shed in the foreground and, barely visible behind it, a tower.

"Ten, nine, eight, seven, six, five, four, three, two . . ."

Everyone leaned forward.

". . . zero."

The screen was instantly blank, not bright, just blank; then slowly from its edges, as though seeping back, the gray of the sky circled in around a light at the center, which in turn began to grow outward against the recovered sky. The circle of light grew to the size of a baseball, darkening at the edges, rising on a column of smoke that ridged and fluted itself as it supported the ball, the ball itself grown smoky, flattening as it moved upward. The horizon was plain again, and to the right of the burgeoning cloud there were three thin streamers of smoke that rippled as they extended off the top of the screen. The wooden shed was gone. The tower was gone. The screen belonged to the cloud, which stood still, or seemed still except for the constant enfolding of smoke shadows at the top and sides, and the constant pumping of smoke into the crown from the column below. The announcer droned on about height, times, size, and the picture changed.

"Jee-zus."

The boys stood up, as though responding to a benediction, and began dressing for the walk to school. Richard pulled on his Levi's, pushing his palms down against his thighs in an attempt to press out the dents the radiator left in the pant legs, scuffed into his half-Wellingtons, and went out the kitchen door. Richard's building was on the edge of the project, across a narrow cinder alley from the ice-house aerator and the canted back staircases of the tenements over the Twenty-fourth Street storefronts. They crossed the cinder lot between the ice house and the chicken plant—its six-foot fan already fluttering pin feathers into the snow—and turned up Twenty-fourth Street, Richard, Gerald, Herman, Reuben, and me.

We headed up Twenty-fourth Street. We picked up Lonnie at the corner, then Balls and Otis at the bottom of Caldwell Street.

"You see that thing?"
"Fuckin' A."
"You know you could carry one a them things in a suitcase?"
"Shee-it."
"'S true, man, don't take no more than a golf ball a uranium to blow up one a them things."
"Yeah, but you gotta have dynamite to set it off. . . ."
"And lead shielding and a graphite and paraffin grid."
"How you know that?"
"Cause I'm a fuckin' spy, man, I know everything."
"Well, all that shit ain't gonna fit in no suitcase."
"Well, they're gonna have one that can fit in a suitcase."
"Damn straight. They got one now they can put in a cannon—the atomic cannon."
"They ain't no cannon can stand no atomic bomb. Shit, man, the whole thing'd get blown up just like that tower today."
"Man, don't you read the newspaper. They got an atomic cannon."

"That don't mean they blow up an atomic bomb in the cannon, dumb-ass. It means that the shell the cannon fires has an atomic bomb inside it."

"Well, that couldn't be much bigger than a suitcase."

"Would you get off that damn suitcase."

"Well, it couldn't be very big."

"Sure it could, cause it's a bigass cannon—biggest cannon in the whole fuckin' world."

"How they gonna shoot a cannon all the way to Russia?"

"Cause it's atomic, dumbass."

"They ain't gonna shoot it all the way to Russia. It's like for a war. They take the cannon to the war, and then they shoot it."

"If it's atomic, though, it means it'll go a long–ass way."

"Fuckin' A."

"You see that mother go off this mornin'?"

"Sure did . . . and I saw your mama go off last night."

"Your mama!"

"Balls, don't start up signifyin', man."

"I ain't signifyin' nothin'. . ."

"Good."

". . . this boy asked me what I saw go off, and I told him. Ain't no signifyin' to tellin' the truth."

"I'm gonna beat your head."

"That's what your mama said."

"Least I got a mama."

"They set one a them things off downtown, it'd kill everybody in the whole city in ten seconds."

"Half a second, man."

" 'Cept if you was behind a hill, then you got a few minutes before the fire gets you."

"There was this Jap in Hiroshima, standin' on a ladder when the bomb went off, and it cooked him away, just like water on a hot skillet. Only trace they found of him was his shadow burnt into the sidewalk across the street."

"No shit."

"No shit, man, just like he had his picture taken by the atomic bomb."

Everyone saw almost every test. The bomb had special properties for us. It was as though it belonged to us by right of attentive devotion, the same devotion that gave each of us a girl, girls hardly spoken to, sometimes fearfully taken as partners in class, but attended to, watched carefully, offered the role of leading lady in the movies in our heads. It is a form of possession or right of first possession, this faithful, diligent kind of fantasy. It was like the way in which we dealt with cars. Each of us had a favorite car—more than favorite, cherished. We were all too young to drive, but we could each describe in great detail the driving characteristics of our favorites. There were arguments—sometimes fights—over the merits of Mercurys, Pontiacs, Chevys, and V-8 Fords. It was important to be extremely detailed, though. There was no point in just liking Pontiacs or Mercurys; specific models and engines were required—Mercury two-door hardtops, Pontiac Catalinas, Oldsmobile Super 88's. Seeing a Catalina on the street could make the day of a Catalina person. "Oh, man, you see that Catalina, aquamarine and cream hardtop, man, with a continental kit?" There were arguments about stick shifts and Hydra-Matics, favored and despised gasolines, tires, camshafts, and seat covers. We could talk one another through the gear changes, cornering, the flatout acceleration of our cars, gargling the street corner idle, humming the engine whine, bubbling the backoff downhill, left wrist hung over an imagined steering wheel, right fist upper-cutting at the shift lever.

Cars were private things, shared in friendship but held close, like jewels cautiously taken into the light, the detailed fantasy exposed so that its particulars flashed like facets. We traded not so much in the known as the partially known, cars we couldn't drive, girls we had barely spoken to, weapons we had no hope of either understanding or acquiring. The details—manifolds, middle names, addresses, horsepower ratings—were what made them real. We lay claim to rifles, pistols, fishing poles, portable radios, outboard motors, even tractors, and knew by heart the jamming characteristics of Browning shotguns, the smooth drag of casting reels, and the edges on German and Belgian hunting knives. None of us had any of this stuff. It was necessary to claim to have fired a wide range of guns. No one had, except, perhaps, Reuben, who had lived in the Ozarks and gone coon hunting with his father. Of course, Reuben used the plausibility of his life as a hunter to create a more extreme story about being attacked by a treed, rabid raccoon which he said he killed with a Boy Scout knife. "You know, the black five-blade with the silver crest on the handle."

Most of our information came from magazines—*Popular Mechanics* and *Popular Science*. It shifted into our conversation, where it accumulated into a broad, fun house, common knowledge, full of exaggeration and misunderstanding. Any information was important, but the stranger it was, the better. A significantly strange bit of technology could steal an object away from its owner. It didn't have to be true, merely convincing. This was jive. Numbers were given to the second decimal point, distances in miles, feet, and inches, and were presented with absolute conviction. At twelve and thirteen, we had independently invented one of the central premises of American advertising—that a product is made valuable by the amount of attention it is given and the precise detail, however fraudulent, used in presenting it. We shaped ourselves by our loyalties to various products in ways the advertisers could never have dreamed.

"That thing scare you, man?"
"Shit yes, man. It's s'posed to."
"Scared the shit outa them Russians, I bet."
"Damn straight."

We turned off Caldwell for half a block, then headed up a steep alley, the first of a complex network of alleys Gerald had mapped into "the alley way," a long shortcut we used to avoid the extortionists along Cummings Street, high school gangsters who muscled younger kids out of their lunch money. At the top of the longest alley there was a haunted house owned by an old *high yeller* woman everybody said was a witch. We threw snowballs at her back porch and a block farther pelted the high walls of a convent. Balls lofted one into the garden that fell at the feet of a statue of the Virgin, and called the convent "Mary's Chicken Coop," after a famous, northside whorehouse, then crowed like a rooster at the iron gate in the wall because he had once seen Singing Sam, the Twenty-fourth Street ragman, falling down drunk, crowing outside Mary's Chicken Coop, shouting, "Mary, Mar-ree, save me!" Reuben said a nun could hex you worse than a witch, and the rest of us moved down the street.

"Nobody ever goes in there, nobody. Somebody brings food or anything, he's gotta put it down by the gate, and that old man lives in that little house over there carries it in . . . and he don't come out neither. One a them dies, they don't go to no mortuary, they just bury her right inside there, in these tunnels that run all under the building."

"If nobody ever gets in there, how'd you know all that?"

"My old man knows this plumber, went in there once to fix the pipes. Had to wear a blindfold right up to where the pipe was leakin', said the whole place stinks of dead nuns. That's why they can't ever sell it. My old man says they take 'em outa their graves and sit 'em up at the table at dinnertime."

"Your old man's full of it."

"He saw this convent in France git blown up by the Germans, and it was full of nun skeletons all dressed up in nun suits, and the Germans ran off cause they knew they was bein' hexed by dead nuns." He put his right index finger in his mouth and wet it to the knuckle, then made a hex's "X" in the direction of the convent.

"Gave 'em boils all over, head to toe. They found this German captain in a ditch by the road screamin' and prayin' for help. Had boils in his eyes, man, and boils on his pecker, too, just cryin' for somebody to shoot him and sayin' like he didn't mean to blow up no nuns. My old man said even his own mother couldn't a recognized him cause of all the boils on his face . . . nose bulged out and crooked with boils and his eyes pushed shut . . . all red and pus-yellow clear into his mouth."

"Did they shoot him?"

"Naw, they captured him, then sent him off to a field hospital. 'Cept there ain't nothin' no doctor can do 'bout a nun hex . . . so he died."

"'Member that kid Jimmy, the one that used to jump out the window when his mother locked him in the house? When he was at St. John's, he pulled the hood right off one a them nuns."

"What for?"

"Cause he ain't never heard Reuben's old man's story about nun hexes, I guess."

"To see if her head was really shaved like they say. Anyway, that's why they sent him to Boys' Town, cause he pulled a hood off a nun. And when they found out, they kicked him outa Boys' Town, too."

"See, even them Boys' Town priests don't fuck with them nuns."

"Was he hexed?"

"Damn straight. They made his ears get all loose and flop down like a dog's ears. Next time you see him, you just look at his ears, how they hang down and shake when he walks, just like a dog."

"Reuben, you're too dumb to be alive. Jimmy got his own ears like that from foldin' 'em down inside themselves."

"Huh?"

"Like this." Gerald lifted his cap and pulled the top of one ear down toward its center. "He'd bend the top down and poke it in the hole, then he'd sit there in class until the teacher looked at him, then he'd wiggle his ears a little and out they'd pop."

15

"What a jerkoff. You mean he fucked up his ears for a dumb-ass trick like that?"

"Point is, Reuben, the way his ears flop around ain't got nothin' to do with no nun."

"What about her head?"

"Whose head?"

"The nun's. I mean, was it shaved off or wasn't it?"

"I dunno."

"Aw, man, you always doin' some kinda shit like this. Start up some story like you know what you're talkin' about, then turns out you don't know shit. That German captain, he probably just had them boils anyway."

"My old man said . . ."

"Your old man? Shit, your old man can't find his pecker if the light ain't on."

"That what your mama said?"

"Naw, that's what *your* mama said."

"That German, he probably got some a that mustard gas and got all them boils."

"Right! That stuff can get inside your clothes, and burn your skin clean off."

"You can be a hundred miles away from an atomic bomb and the radiation can kill you."

"No shit?"

"No shit, and it don't matter if you're in your house or nothin', cause it's just like X–rays. It can go right through anything except lead."

"But it can't go a hundred miles."

"You wanna bet? It can go more than a hundred miles. You can see those Japs, man, from all over Japan, with their skin all bunched up crooked and burnt and people with their eyes gone and babies without arms and legs."

"Man, if it could go a hundred miles, then everybody in New Mexico would be dead right now."

"Maybe they is and nobody's tellin'."

"Aw man, come on, New Mexico is bigger than a hundred

miles. Why do you think they shoot off that bomb in the middle of the desert? Huh? An why do you suppose they have to blow up a hydrogen bomb in the middle of the ocean?"

"What if everybody in New Mexico is dead right now?"

"They'd have to change the signs, you know, 'Welcome to New Mexico—Population Zero.'"

"Ground Zero."

"Right."

"Five, four, three, two, one . . . man, you see that thing . . . just like a fuckin' . . . atomic bomb!"

"Herman, it was an atomic bomb."

"That's what I said, man, that's what I said. Hey Reuben, who's gonna get hexed when the dead nuns get blown up by the atomic bomb?"

"Whoever dropped it."

"I got it. We write a letter to the Russians, you know, and tell 'em we got dead nuns here and they better drop their atomic bomb someplace else if they don't want to get hexed and have boils all over their peckers."

"They're all atheists, man. They ain't gonna care about no dead nuns."

"Nobody ever reads any a them letters you write anyway."

"Yes they do."

"Yeah, what about them baseball uniforms you were gonna get from the bubble gum company. They didn't even answer your letter, did they?"

"I got those Hitler stamps."

"Well, Hitler ain't gonna give us no baseball uniforms. Only time anybody answers any a them letters is when they want you to buy somethin.'"

"I got a letter from the United Nations."

"Sure. 'Thank you for your interest in the United Nations. It didn't say nothin' 'bout sendin' you to all them countries you said you wanted to go to. Anyway, you write a letter to Russia and the FBI'll come and get your ass."

"Fuckin' A, throw your ass in jail for bein' a Communist spy."

"Get away from me man, or the FBI's gonna think I'm a Communist, too."

"The FBI ain't gonna do nothin' just over some letter."

"Wait'll they find out you got a picture a Stalin in your house."

"Come on, man, that ain't Stalin, that's my great uncle."

"With Stalin for an uncle, you'll go to jail for sure."

We turned onto Cummings Street and entered the ordinary school traffic, so we could pass by the malt shop, a vestige of the school's failing link with the middle class. Eventually the building itself would be pushed over by highway improvements. In the afternoon it was packed with customers for malts and sodas; mornings, it was a place for serious coffee drinkers, high school seniors mostly, working at being adults. It was an artifact of another world, another class, a passing era. Cheerleaders in furry sweaters preened over danish pastries; their boyfriends in earnest cardigans and sport shirts buttoned to the neck practiced looking like men with irreversible morning habits. When he reached the malt shop windows, Herman began singing a cartoon cat version of Cab Calloway—

Is you is or is you ain't a Commie?
You is, you is
Is you is or is you ain't a Commie?
You is, you is

with Balls and Reuben singing a do-waa, do-waa chorus of *you is*'s to a confused audience of malt shop teenagers. The cheerleaders looked away; the boyfriends tried to be menacing. Herman, his face gleaming with the coat of Vaseline his grandmother made him use on cold mornings, his hair coiled up into a pompadour sparkling bright beads of melted snow on thick pomade, cakewalked as he sang, and Balls and Reuben, arm in arm, followed a few steps behind.

Is you is or is you ain't a Commie?
You is, you is
Is you is or is you ain't a Commie?
You is, you is

One of the boyfriends started up out of his booth but let his cheerleader coax him back with her butter knife. He was certain that he and his girl had been insulted somehow. We could see him explaining it to her. He said something into the glass at Richard. Herman and company were far ahead, performing for another couple. Richard stopped, leaned close to the window, and said, "Your mama," into the cloud the boyfriend's remark had left there.

At the traffic light Lonnie pointed up the hill and said, "You see that school? Now, watch this. Five, four, three, two, one . . . ba-whamm. Gone, man, just gone."

The thinning snow whirlygigged around the corners of the gray bleachers at the side of the white football field. At the crest of the hill the dark red brick high school was undisturbed.

"Right."

I am not now, nor have I ever been

Several years ago I traveled up the Hudson River from New York to spend part of a day with a gentle old man I had met just a few months before—a poet, ex-expatriate, and old-line American Communist, once even a *Daily Worker* editor. I took a morning train from Grand Central Station, managing the staircase on the Park Avenue side with studied determination, as though there were a camera up in the high ceiling somewhere that was following me through the crowd. A red Mustang was perched on a carpeted platform, spotlighted on all sides, with fluorescent lights brightening its interior toward something resembling the glow of a photograph in a *Life* magazine advertisement. I made it to the gate—Cary Grant fashion—without faltering once, my overcoat open and a *New York Times* neatly folded under my arm. New York City— and especially Grand Central Station—was a test I still had to work hard to pass.

During the train ride I picked at some papers I had with me, ruffled the *Times*, and daydreamed across the patchwork of melting snow out the coach window, hazed with city grime and spotted with rust-water from the rails. My friend met me at a Lionel train set station, and after a few opening enthusiasms and some talk about the bright, unexpected warmth of the day, we walked to his station wagon. We drove through the town and up into the hills along a stretch of blacktop that was flanked with silver birches and occasionally cornered sharply around dramatic outcroppings of black stone.

We had a fine day talking back and forth between the living room and kitchen of his weathered country house. Early in the afternoon he said that he needed a rest and suggested that I might like to take a walk in the hills. I borrowed a pair of high gum-rubber boots and set off through the deep, slushy snow. I crossed the highway, climbed the escarpment that bordered the road, and stood suddenly on the rim of a deep valley, cut down the center by a running stream. After years away from it, I am still enough of a Nebraskan to be surprised, awed, and somehow discomforted by the rocky, wooded landscapes of the Northeast. The silver birch, the dark outcroppings of granite, and the snaggled brush that poked up through the melting snow were features of a country I had never really known, yet possessed instinctively. It is a patriotic hue in the stone or the crosshatch of scrub brush along the cut of the stream, a cultural *déjà vu* that suggests indigo homespun, the punk of watered potash, a flash of Mohican and Delaware through the trees, so different from, yet strangely connected to my long sense of the prairies and the Sioux and the Pawnee. This was the America of colonial movies and James Fenimore Cooper, the landscape of schoolbook histories' fancied revolutionary pastoral—even in winter, the ample land. As much as the West has shaped our dreams, it does not contain this anterior setting, the blue haze that overlays the snow, an imposition of weather and fancy. My country was Dorothy's from *The Wizard of Oz*. This was Hawkeye's.

It was one of the few times in my life that I have felt like an appropriate character for a modern novel, making tracks down that colonial hillside from the porch of a once famous Communist with the veneer of literature wearing away as I went. Over grapefruit juice and vodka laced with anisette, there had been a brief disagreement over the use of names in one of my poems. "Don't you understand," I said, "in a mixed neighborhood like the one I grew up in you never used nicknames unless you were asked, and you were never asked."

Out in the snow, in the glow of that patriotic light, the disagreement pressed back at me as though I could align my more recent sense of the masses and that light into a superior sense of indigenous American politics—an insight that came and went quickly, like one of those fully developed brilliances you wake from a dream wishing you could quickly write down. Communism—my friend had become something of a pasteboard in the hastiness of an ingenious notion—somehow always misunderstood the peculiar aggressiveness of the American proletariat—the serious use of full names among the children supported by ADC in a Nebraska housing project and Hawkeye's arrogance with his British employers, never once assuming social equality but inevitably asserting personal superiority.

Each September brought a fresh group of young teachers down to our crumbling 19th-century schoolhouse, with cast iron hitching posts next to the foot scrapers at its doors, and, invariably, they would read through the class lists, guessing at nicknames, trying to make friends and collecting, instead, rooms full of enemies. My friends and I went to see a brusque, overweight lady Communist in front of the courthouse in Omaha and heard a long speech about the problems of agricultural workers. Everyone walked away. No one in Omaha would admit to having anything to do with agriculture.

My identification with the Yankee landscape was clear: there was a point past which I could not press my alienation and still retain a necessary measure of savvy, woodcraft and lore. Self-reliance, at its best, is a hedge against all possible situations, a predetermined aggression with a handy back door left purposefully ajar. Hawkeye, in woods like the ones I was walking, played his Indian lore against the social presumptuousness of the whites and played white technology—the long rifle—against the Indians. In Nebraska we played our soil against the artificiality of the East and, at the same time, played our traffic jams and proudly, but with convincing horror, wedged our crime rates against any suggestion that we were countrified. In other contexts this process is called *Indian-giving*. I had given years of rhetoric to the Left but was always willing to take it all back in a flurry of chauvinism, was always capable of assailing the theoretical purity of my napping friend's political position with a snippet of lore. It made sense that the New Left had been composed primarily of middle-class and upper-middle-class students. They were the only groups for whom the disguise of proletarianism was a sufficiently interesting lie; for them it could be, as it never could be for a worker on the line or a housing project castoff, an aggression rather than an identification, style rather than class.

The previous August in Chicago's Grant Park I had waltzed with my wife and a friend through two of the worst days of the confrontation with the Chicago police and the National Guard with never more than a whiff of tear gas, staying in the middle of things, but always carefully avoiding the enclosed situation—the box canyon or narrow pass. Swirls of demonstrators in retreat from one National Guard line would collide with another, with an occasional poster figure stopping to shout, "Make a stand at the fountain!" or "Hold the bridge!" before they were eddied away. When my wife and friend decided to walk up to a line of guardsmen who were wearing gas masks and rubber suits and carrying double cannister backpacks of tear gas with large spray nozzles pointed our way, I caught them both by the arms, and we walked down an escape route I already had fixed in my mind. I excuse myself now by saying that it was conditioned behavior, but I have not shaken the sense that in the face of the revolution I had been talking about for so long, I was not capable of the singlemindedness required of the pick-up soldiers of the people's revolution. It was a replay of many earlier situations, more quotidian than historic or spectacular, a street scene with a slightly higher noise level, which I had played many times before.

My father, who had lived in the streets on his own from the time he was eight years old and who rarely left the house without a gun, told me when I was five, "Never fight when you can run," and, "Always hit first and with a stick if you can find one." My father's friend, Grogan, a long time clubfighter and professional sparring partner, said at about the same time, "Guys what don't want to shoot people don't become cops." Years later, on the occasion of our arrest for breaking and entering, after we had, quite innocently, fallen through the roof of the storeroom of Crosstown Liquors, my Indian friend, Russell, said, "If you want to tell a cop to go screw himself, wait till after he's gone." These are matters of woodcraft and lore. The most heroic of what happened in Grant Park happened in the absence of such learning—occasionally, though certainly not in my case, in spite of it.

It was plain that with a bit of study, those Hudson River Valley woods could be used as though they were streets and alleys, as easily as my childhood friends and I had substituted the streets and alleys of the projects for woods. The essential strategies were the same. The terrain was for darting and dodging in and out of, for their entrapment and our escape. Gerald could go out to the left, staying low until he reached the thick overgrowth on the far ridge. Phillip would go right, heading down the watershed to the creek, just where the heavy trees clustered. Everything would depend, as always, on Unca's speed and Chingachcook's stealth. If the French army or the police appeared, we would fade into the brush. My friend, the Communist, slept on the hill, like a storekeeper in a nearby fortified settlement or someone's trusting mother who had sent her son out to play, meaning tag or catch or blind man's buff.

How strange to think that in his day, in my childhood, he was one of the monsters who troubled the sleep of the adult world, a member of the International Communist Conspiracy that was going to overthrow this country by sedition and force of arms. That gentle old engaging poet was once presumed ready to ensnare our youth, steal our secrets, infiltrate our defense plants, ply our homosexuals, and, if necessary, blow up our towns.

I sat down on a dry overhang of rock halfway down the hill and let the mixed old friends and Indians battle the French police below, watched the plan pay off as Gerald and Phillip came up from behind, imagined an overlay of red brick projects, the asphalt plazas and concrete alleys, and the fenced-off garbage cans, always good for an ambush. I packed a snowball and tried to side-arm it across to the next hill. It fell short.

The threat of International Communism had been the companion of much of my childhood and my entire adolescence. In school we were assigned essays on the virtues of the free enterprise system; in church, I listened to accounts of despotic atheism. I stood in line for four hours in a freightyard to get on board the Freedom Train, only to be elbowed past the Declaration of Independence without a close look, and watched each day as fat black arrows filled with North Koreans and Red Chinese pushed out of Manchuria on the newspaper's front page map of the Korean War. We learned the words to "Old Soldiers Never Die" and the language of loyalty oaths and the Fifth Amendment, the flat of Los Alamos, the flat, sandy breasts of Bikini Atoll, and the TNT ratings of stategic and tactical nuclear weapons. Communism, the takeover, the Russians, the Red Chinese, the Bomb, Quemoy and Matsu were among the childhood terms of my generation, entirely woven into what we did, as though they were natural features of the snarl of things we call awareness.

The red menace and its consequences infiltrated everything. It was a presence that occasionally came explicitly close. At one point every head of a housing project household was forced to sign a loyalty oath. In 1950 my grandmother wrote from Germany that it was widely known there that the atomic bomb was kept in long low brick buildings in Omaha, Nebraska. A visionary nun in France, whose feet and palms bled for three hours every Good Friday, said that by 1952 "no stone will rest on stone." American democracy, the Church, baseball, freedom—they all seemed to exist precariously in the face of Communism, strangely defined by their opposite in the way that polio seemed to define walking. By various reports, the movies, the army, defense plants, colleges, and unions were filled with Communists. It was something that threatened the wrong kind of success, the malignancy of presumptuous learning, like the snobbishness we knew was the source of the Communism in movies like *My Son John.*

When my mother went to the housing office to sign her loyalty oath, she said, "You know, if I were a Communist, I'd sign this quick as anything," and laughed. She was told that it wasn't funny and that she shouldn't make jokes. Communism, they said, was not a laughing matter.

Separated from its nightmare countenance in movies and sermons about atheism, it made very little sense. Very early on—in 1948 or '49—I asked my mother what Communism was. She said it was like the first Christians; everyone sold all his property, and the money went to the poor. Afterward, everything was owned by everybody. That made it personal at least. After all, it was Ananias, who had promised to sell all his goods and give the money away, then stashed the money and lied to Saint Peter about it—Ananias whose name has dogged me through years of Sunday School.

Nothing could play so much a part in the lives of a generation—beginning for me at about the age of eight and lasting into college—without growing ambivalent, especially as it passed through the deciduous complexities of adolescence. When I was in my second year in high school I decided to become a Communist, read the *Communist Manifesto* in the only form in which it was allowed in the school library, a book of several hundred pages that surrounded Marx's brief text on all sides with capitalist counter-arguments, and read, or rather paged my way through, *Das Kapital*. My first high school term paper was on the Russian Revolution, the second on peace through world government. I signed my letters and my home-work with slogans about the rise of the working class and inscribed my yearbook, "Workers of the world, unite! You have nothing to lose but your chains!" A few of my friends did the same. We became sentimental Communists, in part, I am sure, because it was so outrageous, but also because any scheme that would take away property and divide it evenly would put all of us ahead, since none of us had any property. We were attracted to Communism in much the same way we had always been attracted to the Brooklyn Dodgers, not because we knew the Dodgers—none of us had ever seen a major league game—but because we instinctively hated the Yankees. However real the Communist threat sometimes seemed, however terrifying its manifestations, Communism in America was a bum's game. In newspaper cartoons Communists were monsters; in actual newsphotos, bona fide American Communists always looked like somebody's unemployed uncle, just a twist of fate away from Ebbets Field and glory. The anti-Communists—the Yankees—had everything on their side, as always. By their own account, all they really had to do was keep the rest of us awake.

In one sense I was a natural for the Party had the Party been the least bit interested. Despite the legend in my yearbook, I was raised not so much in the working class as in the welfare class. My father's long, losing fight with tuberculosis began after an industrial accident in which his spine was fractured. The X–rays taken of the back injury provided the first evidence of the TB he had carried since he was eight or nine years old. He was never properly treated for the disease. In the last year of his life he was refused admittance to the state tubercular sanitorium because during a previous stay he had conducted a protest over food and hospital conditions and had threatened the hospital supervisor with a ball peen hammer. Most of the men in my father's family were laborers; many had seasonal jobs. Those who worked indoors were subjected to regular layoffs. During my father's illness and for years afterward we lived in the Logan Fontenelle Homes on 'Aid to Dependent Children'—small money, hard times, and the regular gawk and occasional tyranny of case workers and housing project officials.

It was not that I was unserious about Marx and Communism. I was quite serious. Marx aimed the whole of history into the Logan Fontenelle Homes and onto my front stoop. The conditions of my life till age fifteen stopped being merely embarrassing and began to serve a rather grand set of historic inevitabilities, which seemed to propose me as one of the heroes of the oppressed. He had not purged the guilt I felt at being poor—the roots of guilt are deeper than politics—but he gave me a way of being aggressive about it and offered me a set of clichés with which I could explain my growing distrust of the Church. The wrongness of my life was no longer simply my fault. It was the fault of the capitalist system.

Still, as suited as I might have been to the Party, I would not have made a good Party member. However earnest, Communism was another dodge, a device to be used when it was handy. It never seemed to be inconsistent that in addition to being a Communist, I also intended to be rich and famous. Both were involved with being different, so were parts of the same strategy of escape, though at one point I tried to join the Party. During the McCarthy hearings so much was made of being a card-carrying member of the Communist Party that I decided to get a card. There was no one in Omaha I could imagine issuing one, so I wrote to an address in New York for what the local paper had called "a well-known Communist front." The letter was never answered. At the time I was angry and confused at not being able to enlist. It was like sending in a box top and not getting the decoder ring. Now it seems characteristically absurd that the powerful organization that was minute by minute stealing away the youth of America, Pied Piper fashion, could not be reached by someone eager to join.

Still, as my mother was told, "Communism was not a laughing matter." It had a biological correlative in poliomyelitis, which bred the same fear of contact and association that Communism created. There were hot days in my childhood when the plaza in front of my house was as deserted as a ghost town, although the four buildings around it housed at least 150 children. We were discouraged from going out in the middle of the day, from playing games that involved physical contact, from swimming, from sharing food or drinking tepid water. So little was understood about the disease that it was susceptible to whatever rumors were available season to season. Paralytic, disfiguring, and deadly, it was the shared nightmare of parent and child, an early initiation to a fear that had a name but no discernable substance, a malady that settled on the young in such random patterns that almost anything could be given as a cause. One friend caught the disease because she was fat, another because she was thin, one because his house was dirty, another because his parents were old. Contact was the most favored cause. The surest way to remain clean and healthy was never to join anything. This was the message McCarthyism offered as well; if you wanted a clean record, it was best not to join any group that had a social or a political purpose, however remote.

The fifties was a fearful era in which the war—always World War II—was made to seem delightful. Whenever the adults in my family rhapsodized most convincingly, they were talking about the war years, a time of spontaneous friendship. Listening to them on Sunday evenings made it seem like a great round of dancing—nights at the Cave Under the Hill, dance bands at the Paxton Hotel or the Fontenelle, parties at the Trocadero and the Colony Club. It was almost unfortunate that the Bomb had made World War III unthinkable. Korea was an unpleasant business that gave us no fashions, no music, no parties. It was not an adventure capable of great common purpose. Limited warfare involved social and mythological restraints. Korea's best movie, *The Steel Helmet*, was a cold, bitter thing that offered neither love nor stardom.

My friend the aging Communist and I had shared the decade at the dipoles of its electricity. He was, presumably, the cause of one of its greatest fears. I was one of his intended victims. Neither of us had played our parts as assigned. He was no villain, and he could never have matched the image of either the crafty ideologue or the heavy-handed, bumbling Russian agent. He seemed in 1968 much more likely to catch the contagions of young minds than spread a contagion of his own. He could only have been the occasion of those nationwide fifties nightmares when he was wholly disembodied in a list waved over a mad senator's head or abstracted in an FBI tally of subversives. I am not doubting the singlemindedness of his Marxism. He had stayed in the Party through its worst years and suffered immeasurably for his convictions. In 1968 he met with more grace than most of the Old Left, the strange, political behaviors of revolutionary youth movements. He approached them as a poet, not as a politico, exhilarated by their jostlings of tone as well as by their hankering after the revolution of his dreams. The grace of his household, his generosity, and his gentleness were so deeply rooted in his character that he confirmed my sense that the red scare had little or nothing to do with actual reds. My friend on the hill became a Communist because for him it had been the only alternative his compassion and injured humanism could take. Keeping the faith was a matter of loyalty and friendship, a fair tribute to the suffering of so many of his friends who had been blacklisted and ostracized. I admired him, but I could not think about him without thinking that it had all been a waste. It was a judgment that came, I think, from my continued dislike of extreme positions and that had its roots in a deeper, pre–intellectual duplicity. My problem was that I wanted to like him more than my own impulses would let me.

I walked back up the hill and crossed the road to the house. He was awake and had a fresh pot of coffee waiting. He asked if I had found anything interesting along the way. I knew he meant, in spite of himself, anything poetically interesting— "one impulse from a vernal wood," even in winter. I showed him a handful of rocks I had picked up for no particular reason on my way back to the house and went on somewhat awkwardly about the geological base of the landscape thereabouts. It proved an inadequate substitute for the sublimity he had obviously hoped for and a poor cover for the mixed politics the countryside had surfaced in me. The remainder of my visit was distracted. Even the train ride back to the city faltered. The first train I was on slowed as it went, finally dying beneath me like a worn horse in the desert. All the passengers were hustled off the train and told to wait on a small platform for a replacement commuter. It was one of America's new blank spaces, the arterial slough of some suburb or another, with the river not far off but unseen.

Back in Grand Central Station only the advertisements that circled the great hall were bright. Centered in the dingy station, the Mustang gleamed, haloed by its circle of floodlights, the figure of the conquering diety presiding over one of the last surviving temples of the locomotive. In alcoves off the terminal's knave, rows of high-backed, uncomfortable benches faced their various clocks, like pews in the chapels of a great cathedral—remnants of an earlier contract with the machine, a symmetrical fancy involving the timepiece, the far-flung system of rails, the corportation, and the polity that now seems slightly comic. The Mustang, by virtue of its name and the wild horse embossed in its chrome decor, its dash of sports-car individualism and its mass production egalitarianism, had no need to diagram its pre-eminence. Parked there on a platform of plush green carpeting, it was a reminder that each commuter line ends in a parking lot, that the collective journey had become merely a brief concession to the city's snarl, and that out there in the middle distance waited an anarchy of Mustangs, Cougars, Barracudas, and Darts.

It was as if I had spent my day jostled between two pasts, my own and my friend's, one almost irreconcilable with the other, although for a time they had shared the same calendar. As fully articulated as the politics that could have resolved the confusion have been, they were scattered by the actual energies of the day. What persisted in my mind as I headed for my hotel was the flashy arrogance of that red Mustang in the train station.

"i do not know this sadness . . ."

There is a haze at the edges of it all, a green haze where the fields trail off toward the sky and trees thicken like sediment. The road cuts slightly into a low rise, barley waving at both sides, occasional thickets, here and there a stand of low trees. The scene is mostly flat and moist. Clouds mount westward, and sunlight falls across the fields in patches. A woman with seven daughters. They pass through the cut in an uneven line. The girls are carrying small pails of berries, and their aprons are stained bright purple. The youngest loiters, scuffing her toe at a clump of broomsedge between wagon ruts. Her fingers are stained; so are her teeth. Her apron is black at the knees, blue-black from kneeling among berries fallen on wet soil. The mother sends one of the older girls back to catch the youngest by the hand and pull her along. They are swinging the little pails and singing, braids jostling to their gait, rough brown dresses and stained aprons rising and falling.

It is one of those scenes you contrive out of a scant story that is told over and over, just a few words really. My mother said that she could remember afternoons of berry-picking with her mother and her sisters, never much more than that, and this landscape devised itself, a small self-contained thing like a painting glazed into the bottom of a shallow dish, the flat countryside near Bremen held in tidy pastoral.

They stop awhile, and the mother sits by the side of the road on the cut's slope. The younger girls clamor around her. The older three cross through barley to a beech-tree, gathering nuts in their aprons. She smoothes back her hair, adjusts one pin at the side, and pats the base of the braided bun at the back of her head. The girls drop fistfuls of wild flowers in her lap—mother-of-thyme, bachelor buttons, and thistle rose. She strips the leaves off the flowers' stems, then twists them together until the blossoms are woven into a garland, which she holds up to her neck. Beechnuts are spread over a small cloth she unfolds on the ground at her side. There is some sorting, then the cloth is knotted at the corners, and she stands, brushing her apron down against her legs with both hands.

I can see her working at a piece of quilting or hooking a rug, her hands gnarled like fruitwood, the way she pulled the yarn through the doubled fabric and knotted it up close or the bright twist of mixed patterns spiraling out from her lap. Out the window just behind her a large neon moon face is flicking the corners of its mouth up into a smile. Beneath it, the words *Murphy Did It* flash on in sequence. Her work table is there at the window, small steel mold, wood and bone instruments, the jar of amber glue, felt pads and circles of transparent animal membranes she works into valve pads—she calls them buttons—for clarinets and saxophones. The sign darkens, then it begins again—face, stammering smile, *Murphy Did It*, its red light on the polished roofs of the cars it was meant to sell like the light from paper lanterns breaking along the soft peaks of rippled water somewhere a long way off.

The wagon road winds toward a town, the needle spire of its cathedral poking through the mist. There is a house nearby, whitewashed at the corner of a small farmyard, with animal stalls at the ground level, the family's close quarters above. The man who waits there—my grandfather—coughs his days away, claws his breath down at the barbed-wire twisted spirals of green stench he sucked into himself on the Western Front. It bites in and burns. They will find him hanging above a toppled milking stool, brightly framed against the milking stall's whitewash, blueberries scattered on the goat-stained floor, wildflower garland dropped there in accidental memorial.

They were held at Ellis Island, my grandmother and two daughters, because the immigration officials were confused by the similarity between the name of the dead father and his brother in Nebraska, the one she had agreed to marry in an exchange of letters, a black sheep she had never met who had to cross half a continent to prove there was a difference between the quick and the dead, Ellis Island, where names were jostled about freehand by clerks dizzy from the rock splash and eddy of tongues all around them. My mother remembers a large, high-ceilinged room, channeled with hand rails, and another small room where she slept in a white iron bed.

Bits and pieces. My old flannel shirt, strips of a housedress she wore for cleaning, remnants of the curtain that had covered the door of the closet in my room in the housing project—she is gathering it all up, hooking and twisting, slowly spiraling it out across her knees. She whistles a thin, falsetto *Lorelei* through her false teeth, turns the rug slightly, palms pressed flat against it, hands stiff with age, spotted, always somehow ceremonial. It is a shoal of pasts—hers, mine, the family's. There are tatters from Weimar in there, scraps from the skirt she wore to Bremen her first day boning herring, a widow miles from home, a few threads of muslin stained with blueberries, northeast Nebraska dust in a linen handerchief, all knotted in and turned. I would sit with my chin on the back of a chair and watch her work the rug, then cross to the table at the window, red *Murphy Did It* neon flicking along the wrinkles at the corners of her eyes, small bone instrument working glue and membrane down against the hard backing of a saxophone pad. She would blot up the excess glue with a damp cloth, then hook the finished button out of the mold and drop it into a canvas money bag, a soft coin saved for deposit at week's end over the counter of the small music company she worked for.

When her brother-in-law/husband died of a stroke, she moved to Omaha to live with the elder of her two American daughters and her husband in an apartment over a commercial building owned by *Murphy Did It*. When I spent the night there, I slept in her bed. She would fluff me into the feather bed, and I would lean against one of her down pillows and watch her unwind her hair, pulling out the long hairpins and letting the braid unfurl down her back, then she would open it out, turn by turn, till it was loose and waving dark gray, covering the back of her robe, enameled yellow brush pulled through it again and again.

"Tell me about Germany."

"What do you want to know?"

"Everything."

"Everything, of course, everything. . . . It is green there. Green everywhere."

"Tell me about the berries."

"There are blueberries and blackberries. They grow at the sides of the road, and flowers everywhere."

"Say something in German."

"*Gute nacht.*" She turned off the light and settled in beside me, pulling and fluffing the cover until it suited her. *Murphy Did It* blinked at the edges of the shade, coloring the room, intermittently tinting her hair. She smelled of field flowers from the cachets she gathered and dried each summer, and of soap. I was a little afraid of falling asleep next to her, so watched the light on the shade, thinking hard about the smile that flicked outside and listening for the deep sound of my aunt's wooden clock. How old was I then? Five, maybe six. And I was afraid of her dreams, something in her immense quiet, the taint of dried flowers on her bedclothes—I'm not sure—that could gather me away from myself into another world, something I would never wake out of, a soft gray-green algaed water unfurling toward me like hair.

It was 1944 or 1945 and the papers each day were full of the destruction of Germany. She had other grandchildren, some old enough for the *Wehrmacht*, a son-in-law in the SS, another who was a Nazi Party official, four surviving daughters nearly twenty years away in a green haze dotted with berries, her brothers and sisters, their families, an unimaginable maze of relatives so complex that neither my mother nor my aunt could explain it, all of them under American bombsights. She had been anti-Nazi from the first. To her, Hitler was a mesmerist who had hypnotized the German people. Very few Germans were Nazis, she said, holding that green vision of hers against the vivid rubble of the newsreels, against the gratification of the hatred of Germans that welled up all around her. My fear may have been touched by the war and the virulence the word *German* was given in American speech then, but I think, instead, that it was the sheer force of an imagination that held its green so firmly and the way it suited everything else about her, the deliberation with which she accomplished herself each day.

The brother-in-law she married had bought a house in a small Nebraska farm town for the family he had agreed to, by mail. There was space for a garden and chickens. He had a harness shop on the town's main street where he fixed horse collars and made the leather belts that drove saws and steam combines, a strange, quiet man who had been in America since he was a boy. Miner, lumberjack, homesteader, farm worker, he had moved around the continent just to see what it was like. "Footloose" is what he was called. He had a packet of stock certificates from bankrupt companies from Minnesota to Washington that he kept for memory's sake in a box with photographs and broken, ironcased watches. He and his new wife lived at some distance from each other, content. The older of the two girls, my aunt, was never really comfortable in his house. She was a teenager. Shy by nature and confused, she harbored a reasonable but unnamed bitterness, a sense of having been wronged that her rectitude and caution would never let be spoken. She left for Omaha as soon as she could. My mother was just eight when they landed in New York, and she accepted a place as her uncle's daughter, allowing the vertigo of the ocean voyage and their detention to foreclose all but a few images of an earlier, green life in another world. They lived through the end of the dust bowl and the Depression in reasonable security. There was little cash anywhere, but there was barter, and they managed rather well. The harness shop had a back room with a potbellied stove. The farmers would gather there in the winter to talk politics and hard times. It gave the harness maker a special place in the town. His wife kept the house and garden. She learned English from Sunday comics, radio, and occasional movies. She was comfortable without ever entirely feeling at home. Her closest friend was an Austrian aristocrat named Rhea, who had married a German farmer she met in New York to spite her family, an even more thoroughly displaced person, who stared at the brown plains from her farmhouse window like a cruel penance. They consoled each other, though one had left death and poverty for comparative comfort and the other had discarded wealth for what must have seemed a bitter austerity. They talked about the brownness of the land and of its waste. My grandmother was offended by the bareness of Nebraska; she never passed a railroad track without complaining that the right-of-way went uncultivated.

Rhea had learned fortune-telling from Gypsies when she was a girl and could lay out the cards with immense conviction, the pack caught in her left hand like a snake's head, the right hand hesitating over each turn—a long pause, then the quick definitive slap, each face registering in her glance, her apprehension mounting like a weather front in the distance, cloud by darkening cloud. When four rows had been turned, she would talk her way through the portent of each card, drawing her fingers along taut, imaginary strings that marked the relationships between them like a musician stroking strange melodies from an exotic instrument, playing card against card into a reading whose complexities seemed to absorb her more than the future she had set out to tell. The first brooding presence of a knave, a darkling suit, all portent dissolved into intricate, self-delighting song, enhanced by her Viennese accent and touched by memories of Romanian summers on the lower Danube with her father. My grandmother's sense of magic was more domestic and immediate. All the remote parts of her life were woven into a single, seamless present that she held to her like a piece of handwork. She could feel the slightest disturbance in the fabric. Death, disease, sorrow, all touched her at the exact moment they occurred. The letters that came later were merely confirmations of what she already knew. The night her brother died she saw his face at the kitchen window; the illnesses of German grandchildren stirred in her fingers as she worked, and the bombings broke over her like shock waves. That green vision of hers was a tightly woven thing, something made by hand that needed mending. As soon as the war ended she applied for permission to return to Germany.

It took years of paperwork, the official Armistice, and thousands of saxophone buttons before she was able to go. The day she left we were all driven to the railroad station, the pillared, weather-stained Burlington. We took turns posing for photographs with her on the platform. I remember my sister with hair ribbons and white ankle socks, my grandmother's dark blue Sunday coat with the brown fur collar, a corsage of gardenias and baby's breath, and the abruptness of it all, like a party that stopped suddenly. Her shopping bags were lifted into the train, and she was gone. She lived in Oldenburg, then Bremen, sent picture postcards, Christmas presents and, for a while, brief notes. She lost her English, or at least her willingness to struggle with writing it. What news there was came through my aunt who could read German.

I saw her once in a dream, wearing her blue coat, walking at the end of that procession of daughters she was herself leading, gathering blueberries fallen from jostled pails. When the family stopped at the side of the road she worked around the edges of the group, tidying the grass, riffling barley crowns with her fingers until they moved uniformly, as though swayed by a soft wind. Back in the stable, she lifted the hanging man down from his noose and folded him into one of her shopping bags, then led the family up a set of rough stairs to a plain kitchen. Everyone had blueberries and fresh milk in small, shallow bowls.

the death of mrs. rich—
a musical interlude

Not long after the war, in the summer of 1946 perhaps, Mrs. Rich, the woman who lived next door to us died. She was an enormous, hulking woman, one of those familiar mothers of seven or eight who wore formless sack dresses that draped unevenly over great thighs. Her hips seemed to stand independently, like appendages or afterthoughts, at her sides; whenever she bent over, even slightly, or walked with especially long strides, they would shift sharply, hiking her dress up over her thighs at the back. This was poverty's own special weight, made of pure starch, affixed to an otherwise strong body like an ever-increasing burden. She wrestled it about when she sat on the back step talking to my mother and heaved at it like a stevedore when she worked. It hung from her upper arms, not flaccid or soft like the fat old age or indolence can put there, but taut and bulging like a goatskin full of water.

Mrs. Rich had eight children by an indeterminate number of husbands. Her two eldest daughters had children of their own which they left for weeks at a time with their mother. Despite their varied paternities, Rich children of both generations looked alike. They were all pale, tallowy in complexion, with blond hair the color of soiled manila envelopes. They had round faces and flat, U-shaped noses. Under more attractive circumstances they would be considered cute. As it was, they looked worn, even in infancy, nearly a dozen of them, oddly indistinguishable from one another, except by age, a scatter of parched squash.

All the serious homemakers on the plaza disapproved of Mrs. Rich and the way she cared for her various children. They just "ran wild," people said, unwashed, ragged, and carelessly fed. Most children envied them. At the first of the month they had potato chips and Popsicles and ate bean sandwiches for dinner out in the yard. In general they stayed up until they wore themselves out, and in the summer shouted at one another under the light on the telephone pole in the backyard, just below my bedroom window. Mostly my mother was troubled by Mrs. Rich's disinterest in the great cockroach and bedbug wars—those weeks in July, usually, when everyone in the eight apartments in our building agreed to fumigate. The idea was to kill the bugs on all fronts. Since Mrs. Rich would never cooperate, the bugs would take sanctuary in her apartment until the DDT or sulfur-bomb smoke cleared away. I remember one night being shaken out of bed by my father, who pulled the mattresses off all the beds and then slopped kerosene over the frames with a paintbrush, while my mother worked insecticide into the buttonholes and seams of the bedding. Then my father went out into the plaza and cursed up at Mrs. Rich's bedroom window. She slept through the whole thing. My mother laid out blankets, and we slept on the floor.

One hot summer night, not the same night, though, Mrs. Rich died in her sleep. She was wheeled off in the morning by four firemen sweating and panting from the struggle they had getting her down the stairs. We all crowded around the door—David, Jack, Johnny, Judy, Victor, Rhoda, Charlene, kids from other plazas, some kids I didn't even know—all pushing to get a look at the body, the green sheet that covered her from head to foot, the gray straps that held her to the stretcher. The cloth over her face was dotted with spots of sweat from the firemen who worked her down from above, dark green marks on the washed-out cotton that seemed rather to have been stained upward from her face, the tincture of death. The adults looked on as well, but from the safety of screen doors held slightly ajar. It was a standard deployment. Children flocked to disasters, running like mad to catch up with fire trucks, ambulances, and police cars, clamoring to get a line of sight into calamity's gaping front door. Adults hung back, guarding themselves with their doors or with small children pressed tightly to their legs.

In a housing project, disaster is a communicable disease that moves, especially in warm weather, like an epidemic. That same summer a disabled marine down the street sat in his kitchen with the gas jets on and lit kitchen matches until the whole room ignited around him, blowing his back door across the yard and leaving him singed but unhurt, sobbing over a small tin kitchen table where, according to just about everyone, his pile of spent matches rested undisturbed. That summer a redheaded woman at the end of my building tried to drown her two daughters in the bathtub because God had told her to. She held them under for a while, then came out into the plaza to tell everyone what she had done in the service of the Lord. The children survived, and she was carted off in the first strait jacket I ever saw, singing "A Mighty Fortress Is Our God." Billy, across the way, pulled a fan off the window ledge into the bathtub and was electrocuted. A girl named Evonne fell down the stairs holding a pair of scissors and drove the point two inches into her ear. Mrs. Danielson began hearing murderers talking through her electric light sockets, then discovered one day while she was waiting to be examined at the clinic that her liver was missing—lost or stolen by her electric murderers. Victor drank a cup of gasoline to spite his grandmother and spent two months in the hospital with hydrocarbon pneumonia. A lady in the next plaza killed her husband with her telephone. An innocent drunk stumbled into Loretta's house by mistake and fell asleep on her couch; when she came back from hanging out diapers, she bashed him with a cast iron dutch oven, breaking her thumb in the process. Fires, scaldings, wife-beating, arms, legs, heads broken, old people and children carried away, sirens and flashing lights all summer long, foot races across the asphalt plaza, up the alley, or down the steps into the street, past the boiler plant to the steel-framed window billowing smoke, hysteria on front porches, snapping at firemen, policemen, sobbing relatives, each other, "What happened, what happened?"

In those early years, playoffs in the city baseball league were held on the project playing field. A crew from the Parks Authority would come down in a dump truck to work the diamond into shape. They would spread fresh clay around and then the dump truck fitted with a drag made of steel beams would circle around and around the infield, smoothing and packing the mound, raising a funnel cloud of dust. It always attracted several children, who would run around with it as though they were chasing one of those playground merry-go-rounds, trying to catch hold of the tailgate chain or get a foot onto the moving drag. The workers tried to shout them away; the kids threw dirt clods at the truck's cab. A boy named Butch who lived on Twenty-second Street tripped at the side of the truck, and his head fell under the rear wheel. Jimmy, who was there, said that he could hear it crack, and Rhoda said the whole truck bounced from it. Butch's body was tangled in the drag. We all rushed to the siren and saw the ambulance attendants lifting him onto the stretcher, his head wrapped tightly in a blood-soaked towel. I remember his mother's head bobbing up and down over the first-base line and the way her fists pounded into her pale housedress just above her knees. There was a hollow in the clay, smooth and round as the inside of a bowl, where his head fell, irregularly stained like half-glazed terra-cotta. It looked as though you could lift it out of the clay it was dented into, gently, with both hands, and carry it away. One of the workmen scraped it full of loose dirt with the inside edge of the sole of his boot, an awkward, childish gesture, as though scuffing at the ground over some rebuke, staring away at the treetops. The ambulance pulled away slowly without its siren on; women huddled over the mother, trying to catch her hands. She slumped, then walked to a police car. Everything turned away from the spot, and the little kids seeped back with twigs and Popsicle sticks, digging frantically at the covered bowl of clay. They were searching for blood and brain, picking at what they took from the hole, probing whatever was dark or moist or soft. "I got me some brain, man!" One of the workmen, the one who had covered the hole, came running back screaming at them, and they moved off.

"Animals!" he said. "Leave it alone." They shouted back, and he started slinging dirt clods to drive them off. They would feint back sharply like dogs, then return. Then they were throwing dirt as well, golf-ball-sized clods. The workman chased one, then another, and the chunks of dirt hailed down on him. "Fucking animals, fucking little animals," he said in retreat, and they circled back to their work. We watched them for a few minutes, digging and scraping on all fours, but didn't participate, not that we hung back from any moral conviction but that theirs was a children's game we were too old for. We watched them just as we had watched what was left of the accident when we arrived. We were out after the event, and these kids panning loose dirt like goldminers had become part of it, happening at the edge of a vortex of broken body, bent mother, and mad workman.

The object was to get to the scene before it was all over, to get a long, close look or just a glimpse of something broken or bleeding, to see the nightstick dent someone's hair as neatly as the heel of your hand can crease a pillow, then watch the blood rise slowly to the surface, the ambulance attendant lift the stomach pump through the door, something, some scrap of it to carry back home, to relish through a week or more on the recreation hall fire escape, anything vivid or terrifying you could catch hold of before all the pieces rocked back into place and the hot air settled in again. The acid spots on Mrs. Rich's shroud smoldered and grew until her eyes looked out blankly.

Mrs. Rich's older daughters put together the money for a funeral but were unable to find any male relatives willing to act as pallbearers, so my father agreed to organize a group from the men in the neighborhood. It was one of the few time six able men could be found for such a chore. From late 1945 through 1947 there were a number of veterans about, resident fathers and sons on percentage disability or the G.I. Bill. The morning of the funeral my father turned out in his usual double-breasted black suit, gray fedora tilted, as always, over his right eye. It was his leaving-the-immediate-neighborhood uniform; he looked like a gambler or a character in a detective movie. The others gathered on our front step, none quite so dark or funereal as my father with his straight, long nose, thin mouth, and sharply angled, tubercular cheeks. From next door there was Preston Johns, father of my friend Johnny Johns, an ex-Seabee; another ex-sailor named Bud, a thin, Sinatra-esque fellow recovering from a head wound you could occasionally see under his black hair; a gregarious old mess officer named Kelly; and two of the Cullen boys just back from the Marines. They assembled soberly, then left for the church in Kelly's black Dodge sedan. Dressed up, hair slicked down, smelling of shaving soap and Lucky Tiger, they descended the plaza stair with what I remember as great ceremony, slowly and in pairs, as though the coffin already rode between them. We followed only after the car doors were shut and trailed up the street after them when the car pulled away.

It was a hot slow day. By noon the plaza was empty. Some of us sat on the back door steps where there was a little shade. For a while we trailed Popsicle sticks through the cracks in the withered yard. All the shades in the building across the yard were drawn against the sun. A few towels and dishrags hung stiffly over the wire clotheslines that stretched the length of each building from evenly spaced T-bars. We sat under the elm tree awhile, picking at the gray bark with penknives and can openers and drank lukewarm water from a surplus canteen David carried on an ammo belt most summer days. Johnny's mother made Kool-aid. The pallbearers were expected home at three o'clock. When my mother called me in for dinner they were still not back. She spent most of the afternoon at the screen door or on the back step with other wives, anxious and angry.

Perhaps it was just Nebraska, a vestige of the prairies surviving whatever else was done to the land, or the peculiar weight of the weather there, the way the sun settles down on everything, or the housing projects themselves, a squat grid of brick buildings with squares of asphalt and parched crab grass alternating between them to make front plazas and backyards, that gave such a dead quiet to summer afternoons like this one. Everything was drawn back behind the uniform yellow shades, and the world was nearly empty. Hot days, we would wander, three or four of us, through desolate places, scuffing at the soft dust that lined the gutters, setting out from the recreation hall fire escape on one of our circuits of the neighborhood. We went by Adler's Bakery on Twenty-fourth and Clark and made fingermarks on the bread cases, hoping that Old Man Adler would give us each a day-old bagel to go away. We stopped to taunt Wolfson at the door of the garage, where he rolled out his rag and paper scale each day. Up the cinder alley behind Twenty-fourth we stood awhile in the fine spray from the ice-house aerator, a house-sized cube of gray louvers where water fountained day and night all year long. There were tenements above all the Twenty-fourth Street shops with skewed gray porches facing the cinder alley that would have been Twenty-third Street if it had been a street. Under the porches there were a row of sheds that ran the length of the tenements from the ice house to the vacant lot on Clark Street where Wolfson kept junked cars. Some afternoons we would run across the roofs of the sheds, jumping from roof to roof like characters in a movie chase, occasionally, though, punching a heel, sometimes a whole foot through the rotted roofing. The noise would bring out one or two storekeepers shouting or waving pistols.

Every day Mr. King sat out on the end of the Franklin Avenue plaza in a kitchen chair, his unimaginably old, black skin glistening like wet bark over the arthritic gnarls of his hands, his face welted all over with gleaming tubercles. We went that way in order to say hello to him, politely and with genuine respect. It was one of the things we did. We harassed Adler and Wolfson, begged glasses of water from Gene at the Decatur Drug Store, ran across roofs, peeked in windows, stole pop bottles from behind the 7-Up bottling works on Twentieth Street and sold them to the grocery store, sat up in the oak tree on Clark and ate Baker's Coconut from a can we'd buy with the proceeds, and politely said hello to Mr. King. He would watch us cross the cinder alley, answer "Afternoon, boys," then watch us till we went around the corner of his building. He sat in state almost, occasionally moving his chair to keep in the shade, his age and the knotted calcium in his joints requiring a slow, ceremoniousness of gesture. He had something in common with Mr. Ciotto, the *compare* in my father's old Italian neighborhood—not the official sanction or family loyalty certainly, rather something of the same manner with which the *compare* took the air every Sunday, as though he were the primary witness to the progress of his world. With the gravity that goes with accepted stations of privilege and responsibility, Mr. King watched over the slow passing of hot, vacant days. When we mourn the loss of neighborhoods, we ought to mourn the banishment of this quiet, sentinel aristocracy, old men and women whose job it was to witness the way things went. Even hemmed in by the buildings on his plaza, Mr. King seemed to preside, if only in manner and the unfaltering duty with which he kept his place. Speaking to him, acknowledging his presence, was important—at least to us; he was one of the few pinnings that place ever had, somehow seated each day on the ground beneath the plaza while almost everyone else flapped and frayed from disaster to disaster like loose bits of a ragged, unstitched quilt. "Yawl know," he said one day, "how they come to build this project here? Use to was all houses and tar-paper sheds." (No way to misspell English into his dialect—antique Mississippi and Omaha black, its consonants detailed everywhere by a lifetime of African Methodist Episcopal pulpit oratory.) "Till the tornado come an blew it all away."

The afternoon of Mrs. Rich's funeral we stayed in the yard. It was past seven when the pallbearers finally roared back, boisterous and disheveled. They laughed up the stairs and into the backyard like a winning team, jostling one another as they walked, arms draped over one anothers' shoulders, backslapping, recoiling with laughter, then regrouping again. My father came into the house and took off his coat and vest. My mother filled a dinner plate, but he waved it away and went back into the yard. The group reassembled, surrounded almost immediately by a dozen children, wheeling around, tumbling, darting back into place like pilot fish, tugging at arms, belts, pant legs, and sleeves. They had stopped for a drink after they "put the old lady away." There had been, they explained several times, an argument about where they should go. Several taverns were suggested, and instead of arguing about it, they went to all of them. It was obviously the best day any of them had had in a long time. They moved around the yard, propelled, it seemed, by their laughter. Sometimes the group fractured and reassembled, and there were occasional sorties to kitchen steps, where the wives watched, nervous and resentful, a little afraid of the size and abandonment of the gestures that were filling the yard.

The Cullens brought out a case of beer. A radio was set out on a kitchen chair, wired through a window with an assortment of extension cords. Slowly the women were drawn out, pulled along by their husbands or caught up as they ran after stray children imperiled by boisterous arms and legs. Florence Johns changed into high heels and a satin dress. There was dancing and cream soda and suddenly a block of ice in a washtub, highballs from pints of whiskey, 7-Up, and bologna sandwiches. Valeeta, who looked like Rita Hayworth and was unattached, danced with everyone and sang. My friends and I took turns shinnying up the telephone pole guide wire just outside Mrs. Rich's door, hanging over to watch it all upside down—agitated beer sprayed up into the lamplight, Bud's wife in baby-doll pumps, Valeeta's auburn pompadour, the arc of the softball two Cullens were tossing just over the hands of several younger boys, mothers dragging babies away from the dancers, jitterbugging, real jitterbugging with legs kicked up high, skirts swirling, high heels caught in cracked soil, grass-stained satin, blouses cut from parachutes out at the waist, precious nylon stockings torn, the lamp above me shaking from my weight on the guide wire, riffling busy shadows. The fathers were all dripping with sweat. Between songs the women lifted their hair up away from their necks with both hands, as though posing for some memorable glance.

The radio played "Let the Rest of the World Go By." Valeeta began singing again, soft and throaty, swaying with the slow beat, her hands clasped at her waist like a choirgirl. All the adults were quite still; several of them were crying. . . .

A place that's known
to God alone,
and let the rest
of the world go by.

. . . as though that were the dream everyone had gone to war with or nurtured carefully as they waited for it all to end and for them, unevenly pieced back together, as down and out as they had been through the thirties, faded like a receding light, the dim yellow wedge of illuminated numbers on the radio's face, the only sunset left to dream themselves into.

The fight started a few minutes after the song ended. Bud's wife blamed her broken shoe on Johnny Cullen's big feet, and Bud swaggered up to their shouting match like a cowboy, hiking up his pants, ready for action. His wife turned on him, telling him to go sit down and remember the steel plate in his head. It was as though she had told him to remember that an explosion had blown away his crotch. He said he would clean up the yard with Cullen, pushed her away, and started swinging. Bud had been a lightweight contender in the Pacific fleet, so was up on his toes dancing, jabbing at Cullen's face with a pretty left. Cullen didn't quite know what to do. Like all the Cullens, he was a giant, taller than Bud by at least eight inches, outweighing him by a hundred pounds. He backed away from the flicking jabs, then stopped as firmly as if he had backed into a wall. With one great lunge of his forearms, he pushed Bud away. Bud's wife was screaming. When Bud fell she fell, too, like a domino neatly placed behind him. She grabbed his shirt and tried to hold him down, ranting on about the plate in his head and how he was going to get killed. He shook her off and started back at Cullen.

Suddenly everyone was in it—Kelly haymaking in every direction, all the Cullen giants, Preston Johns punching up with short quick blows, deliberate and effective like a man at familiar work, Bud dancing and falling, Florence Johns, her satin party dress shredding at the hem, hammering at the back of one of the Cullens with the heel of her shoe, Bud's wife swinging from Johnny Cullen's arm like a monkey on a rope, children tumbling off in every direction like loose dirt from a collision. My father went into the house and came back wearing his vest. My mother tried to keep him out of the yard but stepped aside. By the time he reached Bud and Johnny Cullen they were wrestling on the ground with Bud's wife tangled in their legs. I could see my father's back as he bent down to the three of them. They pulled themselves loose of one another, and Bud and his wife went back to their kitchen door. My father crouched next to Johnny Cullen a few seconds, then they stood up laughing. Kelly and Art Cullen were flailing at each other in the hedge around the garbage cans down by the alley. Preston, the night's champion, was still punching upward from that low, swaying stance of his. Florence, with a high-heeled shoe still poised above her head, was circling, looking for someone to hit. Then, like a brief, feathering wind through street dust on a hot day, the whole thing stopped.

The Cullens sat on their back step and were scolded by their mother, a weathered Irish gnome who ran a northside saloon. On our side of the yard there were recriminations and first aid. Everyone, even the Cullens, inquired after the security of Bud's steel plate. He said that he was fine and that he had been a lightweight contender in the Pacific fleet. There were bloody noses and cut hands. Kelly's face and arms were welted from the hedge. Preston soaked his hands in a basin of ice water. The hotel dance band high atop something in the heart of downtown elsewhere played on. My father was pleased with himself, walked around the yard once, then went into the house and put away his gun. What remained of the case of beer was passed around; it was downed quietly by men withdrawn to their own kitchen doors. The radio was disconnected. Mrs. P. walked out into the middle of the empty yard, dumped the water and remaining lump of ice onto the grass, and carried her washtub home. Two police cars arrived just as I was being sent to bed. "Just having a little fun," my father said, "it's all over now."

In the morning there was a patch of green in the yard where the ice had melted. Everyone was amiable again. The milk trucks dripped their snowy ice up the alley; old man Rosen and his wife came to the bottom of the alley in their pickup truck hawking potatoes, tomatoes, Rosen shouting his version of a New Orleans street call, "Strawberries, berries, berries, strawberries," with Yiddish r's. High Waterpants pedaled off on his tamale cart with his overalls neatly folded up over his socks. Singing Sam, the ragman, scuffed walked-down shoes behind his high-wheeled handcart. Wolfson's scale was out. Mr. King had taken his place. My mother boiled new potatoes and string beans with a strip of salt pork, and the smell of it fell over the yard where my friends and I played The Fight through over and over again. Preston Johns was thought a hero for taking on the Cullens. Nobody wanted to play Bud, who was considered a fool for having started something he couldn't finish. My father held his strange place in everyone's regard, a dark figure who had worn a suit and hat and spent most days he was home in the front bedroom. They knew he played cards and that he had a gun. When he was a boy living in the back room of a southside barbershop, he was called Jesse, after Jesse James. The name seemed to suit him not just because of the suit or the gun or his long, thin face and precise hands but for the way he brooded out of view, alone in the front bedroom or in a remote state hospital I never saw. Jesse James was his favorite hero; I suppose that was the source of the name. He loved to tell Jesse James stories, especially the one about Jesse James and the widow woman. The face I saw in the shadows of the barn, past the barren farmyard where the widow counted out her last pennies to the leering landlord, was always his, and later he was the one who stopped the landlord's buggy on the road and took back the widow's rent, that most hallowed Jesse James, the champion of widows and poor farmers, whose task it was to settle their accounts with landlords, bankers, and the railroads, "The one man," my father said, "who knew what battles the Civil War had failed to fight."

That night at dinner I asked him what he had said to Johnny Cullen that made him stop fighting. "I just told him that it was time to quit before someone got hurt," he said. I wanted to ask whether he had showed his gun but was afraid that he wouldn't like the question. My mother hadn't mentioned the gun, which was back in the green steel box on the shelf in the bedroom closet wrapped in a cotton handkerchief, keeping company with old satin medallions and rosaries, a few documents, souvenirs, and my mother's father's broken pocket watch. I knew neither of them wanted to talk about it because if it came up, there would be an argument; there were always arguments about that gun. He ate the beans and potatoes. It wasn't a dish he had ever liked very much, but that evening he said that they were very good, then smiled and said to my mother, "You know, those guys were just looking for a reason to quit." After dinner we went out and sat on the front step. My mother picked wilted blossoms off the four-o'clocks in the small patch of ground under the front window. Just as it was getting dark my father asked me if I wanted to go for a walk. We went up the plaza and down the alley, then on to Twenty-fourth Street. He bought five loose cigarettes from Old Man Merritt at Decatur Drugs and took me to the fountain and ordered two cherry Cokes.

"How did you know?"

"What?"

"That they wanted to quit."

"Nothing to that," he said. "Almost everybody who gets in a fight wants a reason to quit." He looked at his change and ordered a chocolate ice cream cone for my sister and a strawberry malt for my mother. When she pulled the malt out of the sack, my mother said that my father shouldn't have done it, unwrapped the straw, and pushed it down into the malt with great care, then held the carton in my father's direction. "We've had ours." He pulled a moist Camel out of his shirt pocket, tapping it on his thumbnail before putting it into his mouth. After the others had gone inside, we sat on the step for a while, my father Jesse and I, smashing inch-long waterbugs with a ball peen hammer.

Perhaps fathers who die young are all thus shrouded in odd intensity by their sons. My sister remembers very little of him, and what she does recall suggests a far different character. My brother was too young to have had any part in it. I alone have, then, these islands of clarity, like the evening of the day after the fight where every detail is completely available, the drawer in the oak cabinet from which Old Man Merritt counted out those five cigarettes, for example, or the way my sister stared at the chocolate on my hand as though in addition to stealing him away for nearly an hour I had also managed to steal something precious and irreplaceable from her ice cream cone, the fresh marks of the scoop along the edge and more dear, even, those rills and furrows the chill holds on the surface so briefly. The waterbugs split open with a sharp crack; locusts whined like over-revved engines in the trees.

One day that fall he was outside school waiting for me in a gray Studebaker President. We drove north and east toward the river, then around Carter Lake, a muddy hook of water the river's abandoned course had left behind. He parked the car and took me down to the water. He pointed to a brick water wall that curved under low-hanging branches. "I helped build that wall," he said, "on the WPA." Then he drove all the way across town to Riverview Park, took me to the round lagoon, pointed to another wall and said, "That one, too." On the way home he drove up the steep hill past St. Anne's and showed me how the car could hold itself at the stop sign, even though he had his foot off the brake. It was called hill-lock, and we sat there looking up the long, pointed hood until a Buick honked behind us. He had borrowed the car from someone, and that night after dinner, returned it.

He was always very serious about instructing me, offering bits of information and pragmatic, behavioral imperatives with what still seems, as I think of it, incredible intensity. I never doubted that he borrowed that car in order to show me those two walls, the north and south borders of his part in the city. We were walking his perimeters that day, the boundaries of the place he had only wistfully to offer. One day he sat me down at the kitchen table and showed me his revolver, tracing the crosshatch on the grip for me with great care, turning it in the light to exhibit the bluing on the trigger guard and the snub muzzle; then holding it just above the table, he let the butt fall, thunk, and the whole kitchen seemed to shake. He talked about the real McCoy, the genuine article, and let it fall again, thunk. It was a lesson in the weight and hardness of real things, the real McCoy, as he said. It was one of his obsessions, the spectacular reality presented by the surfaces of finely accomplished things—his gold watch, the case work on our Zenith radio, the leather box he kept loose tobacco in. More than anything, he hankered after a hard lustre in things, the deep burnish of the real in metal, the weight of leather, the flex in a hat brim of Italian felt, as though the catastrophe of his life could be abraded with them.

He left home when he was eight after a violent argument with my grandfather. Occasionally his mother, withering with the tuberculosis he had already contracted, would manage a truce between them, and he would go back but never for very long. He had a shoeshine stand in a Twenty-fourth Street barber shop and slept on a cot in the back room. Sometimes he sold newspapers. He hadn't the stamina for construction or heavy factory work and eventually settled in as a dealer in a back-room card parlor. He lived not so much by his wits as by his sense of style, a demeanor pieced together, I suspect, from the remnants of his southern Italian background, barbershop chic, the mannered precisions of the card table, and the movies. Sometimes, in fact, I can think of him only in the grainy black and white luminescence of the screen, moving at some distance amid the angled gray shadows of a detective film. His collection of friends had to it the strange resourcefulness we expect of Hollywood detectives—two doctors, an ex-club fighter and professional sparring partner, newsstand proprietors, policemen, the near–North Side's flashiest black gambler, stumble bums, politicians.

He also had a fondness for the old Italians, the moustaches. When he made his long streetcar runs around the city he would always stop in the oldest part of the old neighborhood and sit with them playing finger games or nodding "*Sì, sì*" to their drowsy Calabrian rambles, mostly round men with heavy, bent hands who could, my father said, count the pebbles in Italian streets they hadn't seen for forty years. "*Ah . . . Riventinu, coronata di faggi!*" Yes, yes, he would nod, feeding his own melancholy with a nostalgia for a place he had never seen— crowned with beech trees, a gentle mountain not far from the sea. They would all embrace him as we left and run their meaty hands through my hair. He took some of his authority from those sessions with the old men, finessing my grandfather, I imagine, by making his own pact with the old country. In his own mind he was a *don*, and it was the *don* in him that arranged funerals, broke up fights, and made of him such a peculiarly magical teacher.

Southern Italians are by cultural inheritance—perhaps by disposition—necromantic. It is not so much that they love the dead or death itself but that their lives are arranged to move among the dead in ways that give them more than sentimental esteem; they have a tangible presence as well. The habits of mourning among women are taken on for life, swaying a black crepe background to family occasions. Religious services for the dead—not only funerals but regular novenas and masses subscribed to nudge souls out of Purgatory—mingle every-where with a non- (even pre-) Christian magic. Conversation inevitably involves the dead. They play along the edges of late evening pinochle games and are involved in the scenic refer-ence of any nostalgia. That faint wisp of Calabria—beech-trees on a native mountain—had a deathly host in it. Death had its own protocol, a system that gave far greater importance to mortuary visitations than funerals. For distant cousins my father could forego the actual service, but for any relative at all attendance at the mortuary was absolutely necessary. He had to sign the visitor's book and pay for a two-dollar "place." Also absolutely required was the annual gathering of families at the Calabrian community's cemetery on Memorial Day. It began early in the morning and went on all day, with masses said at sunrise, noon, and sunset. They were all there—grandfathers, grandmothers, aunts, uncles, children running fearful games around the corners of soft, tended soil, the old ladies in camp chairs, fresh flowers and groundcover just planted, wreathes and palm frond crucifixes, and flags everywhere, fluttering over the graves of lost children, wives, great-grandfathers. Not only had they pre-empted the national holiday for their own ancient purposes, they had gathered up, as well, all of its emblems for their own. The contest for Memorial Day had to do with arriving earlier than anyone. My father would rouse me in the dark, and we would ride there in an empty streetcar so that he could prop a dime-store wreath on his mother's grave before his father arrived with sacks of flowers and nickel flags. Then we would walk around awhile among the older gravestones on the hill or on the flat where friends and cousins lay. And he would name the ones that mattered as we went and watched as the roadways filled with cars. Old women spooned black soil around seedlings; the old men gathered in their stiff suits; the lineage of children was explained as they crouched behind their mothers. When the preparations for mass on the pavilion on the hill got under way, we would leave. It was an exercise of community, more crucial than a saint's day festival, a time for matters of family to take their public place as history. As incongruous as they seemed decorating the graves of old men and women who never spoke English or children dead before they could speak at all, those flags were oddly appropriate, signaling the American investment of a people who mark time and place with what they bury.

My father's involvement in the burial of Mrs. Rich engaged a role he had always known. The community that gathered that night had no common history and had nothing to open out into the yard for singing and dancing but private family matters, that and a shared sense of loss. If you lived in the housing project, you had been passed over or damaged and left behind. It was a place of closely packed disasters because its citizens were chosen for their skill at disabling calamity. Presiding over disaster—it is what the *dons* have always done best. Mrs. Rich meant nothing to my father except as an annoyance. Her children and roaches invaded his quiet, but her death was the occasion for a briefly contrived community. Even when it collapsed, he cut a good figure. He was like a skydiver capering a bit along the accelerating line of descent, offering the illusion of purpose—that saving grace!—to an environment where the chains of cause and effect worked with too brutal a thoroughness to allow the selection from which plots are made. In less than two years he was dead. My grandfather in search of a last victory—maybe, his only victory—over a stubborn son fought with my mother for control of the funeral. She held her ground. He offered to take me off her hands. She said no. Two days after the funeral without knocking he left two live chickens in a gunnysack on the back step and never entered my mother's house again.

what would you do if this was for real

Air raid drills came in squawks, not the long, familiar rings of the fire bell. *Drratt, drratt, drratt.* Instead of 30 minutes out on the street, it meant filing down into the inside corridors of the building and crouching there with our backs against the gray lockers. There was some terror in this, in part built into the discomfort of it all. Lining up on the sidewalk or scuffing a cinder playground was hardly a disaster, nor was the prospect of standing there one day watching the school go up in flames a matter for special apprehension, but crouched in those long halls with tin louvers jigsawed into your spine made you half-expect a flashbulb pop of light that would jump out of all the doorways, then, perhaps, the whole building coming down through the ceiling, like one of those cave-ins greed and gunfire brings down in played-out movie gold mines. Or the flashbulb more searing, more completely bright, bubbling us all up in its fast heat like the plastic that fits over the glass and hisses for a moment after the light is gone. Light travels faster than sound, and sound we knew was sock moving in air—General Science. So first there would be light, then noise, and with the noise—at the same instant as the noise—the whole building would jump up into toothpicks or smithereens, like that hut in the Los Alamos slow-motion movie everybody knew by heart. *Conlrad's* 15 minutes. "Go to your nearest Civil Defense Shelter (three fan blades on a yellow sign). If you are in your home . . . If you are in your car . . . Await further instructions."

". . . I ever meet a Russian, I'll kick his ass."

"Man, you gonna have to wait in line."

"What was that noise?" Frightened whisper, Herman's.

"What noise, what noise?" Herman, laughing.

"Shut your mouth."

"You gonna shut it?"

"What would you do if this was for real?"

"Steal that fucking 98 and get the fuck outa here."

"Listen to that boy talk, can't even drive."

"Yes I can."

"Shee-it."

"Drive straight up Cummings Street an outa town."

"The best place to be is the basement."

"You talk like a dogassed teacher sometimes, you know that?"

"Well, it's true."

"I don't give a fuck if it's true, shut up."

"I ain't gonna steal no car or climb down in no basement. I'm gonna fuck Ellen Perkins."

"Man, they ain't gonna let you fuck nothin'."

"Who ain't gonna let me. They all gonna be sulkin' around waitin' to get blown up, an' I'm gonna be fuckin' Ellen Perkins."

"You gonna have to wait in line."

"Not for you, peckerwood, I ain't."

"Where you gonna do it?"

"Right there."

"In the middle of the hall?"

"Fuckin' A."

"Jesus."

"You'll have to fight me first."

"I'll run you down, mother fucker."

"You two can fight on, then I'll get her."

"After me."

"If everybody starts fightin', ain't nobody gonna get fucked."

"That's the truth."

"Then we gotta pick different girls, spread 'em out."

"I pick Ellen Perkins an' I'll spread her out."

"You ain't gonna pick shit. I picked her first."

"Wait up, man, we gotta do this fair. We'll write down all their names—only the good ones—an' we'll have a drawing, all right?"

"I don't know, man. It don't seem fair cause I picked Ellen Perkins while dragass here was talkin' 'bout stealin' a car he can't even drive."

"What if we let you pick first?"

"I dunno? It still don't seem fair."

"Come on, man, you fuck this up an' we won't let you pick at all."

"Okay, I'll pick first."

It took the rest of the morning to settle on the list of girls—six of them. The first three were easy; the last three took some serious thought.

"Judy, she ain't got no tits at all."

"Ain't nobody askin' you to fuck her tits."

"What about Shirley then. She's got tits. . . ."

". . . an' pimples."

"Put a flag over her face."

"Come on, man."

The drawing was held at lunch over the setting mucilage of hamburger gravy on mashed potatoes. Everybody bitched, except Gerald, who got Ellen Perkins. Herman got Judy and said he was more fucked over than fucked and, quietly, "Man, you sure you can fuck a girl that ain't got no tits?" Balls, who thought of the whole thing first, bitched because Ellen Perkins was his idea, but he got Connie, who was everybody's second choice and had tits. By the time everybody got back to the table with their banana-Sweden-cream ice cream, a sense of property had developed—even in Herman. Also, Herman felt better after Balls told him that the more a girl fucked the bigger her tits got.

"When I get done with that girl, she'll look like Marilyn Monroe."

What followed was somewhere in between knight-errantship and peeping tomism. Gerald took to opening doors for Ellen Perkins. He would follow her down the hall just so he could open a door for her. He also managed to drop something every time he passed her desk so he could stare up her skirt. Balls drew pictures of Connie's tits everywhere, but called her Constance and said, "Excuse me, miss." The girls were just confused, especially when one of the six came up from behind and said in a strange tone, "The Russians are coming," and ran off laughing.

The connection between the Bomb and sex was there from the start. The strands were played out in any number of directions—power, merely; spontaneous energy; even that mushroom cloud, I suppose, was the great, smoke and dust hard-on of the American desert.

At the far end of the corridor in which Balls initiated that bomb-defying scheme of his was the room where we had our music classes. It was an abandoned commercial arts facility with full-scale shop windows facing the lockers in the hallway and a stock room at the rear. Twice a week we shouted through the Deems Taylor Songbook like Holy Rollers in a storefront church.

> Tell me, where was you
> When the *Titanic* went down?
> Tell, me where was you
> When the *Titanic* went down?
>
> I was standin' on the corner
> Jumpin' up and down,
> Standin' on the corner,
> Jumpin' up and down.

Nobody there, certainly not the short, square music teacher in nubbed tweed, pursing up to her pitch pipe, knew the social content of the song. *"Am. Negro Spiritual"* is what it said at the top of the page, and we sang it, *Am* Negroes and *Am* poor whites, as loud as we could, jumping up and down in our seats, however the teacher tried to quiet us. The reaction to the song frightened her, and she tried to avoid it, the sassy punch and spit that came with the refrain. She wanted to be somewhere else—on another page, in a different school, another country, anywhere. These were afficionados of disaster singing, shouting out with pleasure at that remote catastrophe in the North Atlantic, flaunting at the same time her failure to contain them. She would choose songs that were more subdued. In "Swing Low, Sweet Chariot" Balls would sing "Swing low, sweet cherry ass," and the slow, quiet tune would get raucous. Several of us agreed that the next time we sang "Swing Low" we would all just mouth the second chorus and let Balls sing an unintentional solo. "Swing low, sweet cherry ass," Balls sang alone. The teacher reddened and sent him to the office for punishment. He sulked when he stood at the desk, waiting for the note and argued again that he "didn't do nothin'," but when he got to the door he waved the note and bowed to the rest of the class.

In those days *cherry* meant *virginal*, but anything especially fine, without stain or tarnish, was cherry as well. The word was used most often to describe an especially well kept used car. So Balls's inventive mutilation jostled at least two eroticisms. "Swing low, sweet cherry ass / Comin' for to carry me home." Balls was reprimanded for using an obscene word in class and given another note—this time from the principal—to take home to his mother. The music teacher was both fuddled and angry. I doubt that she understood the range of suggestion set loose in what Balls had sung. The principal probably never knew what was said, just that it had been obscene. Balls's mother was later certain of nothing more than that her son had done it again. For the rest of us it had a shimmering presence, a gesture faceted with unmeasured lust, at once graphic and unreal. "Swing low, sweet cherry ass"—it was like so many of the figures we had for sex, both grotesque and concrete, an ass like a pendulum descending, bright, maraschino, and it was defiant, an inspired vandalism, Balls once again scrawling dirty words on an icon—first, the Bomb, then, salvation.

In that setting music teachers were particularly vulnerable. They had to let us sing, that was the point, but it was like shaking a hornets' nest. Music was close to our defiance, that core of violence even the meekest among us shared—resting with obscenity, sexual muddle, aggression, fear, those nearly habitual claims on each other's mothers—the critical mass rock-and-roll would later play at, explore and, finally, exploit. It wasn't Miss Huebrick's fault things always went badly. She had been pleasant, even eager at the start of the year. You could feel sorry for her under constant assault. One afternoon she passed out a form on which we were supposed to evaluate her class. The room was quiet, strained. Nobody had ever asked anything like that before, and the forms were completed slowly, with a tentativeness that hardly went with the setting. Balls made a great show of writing his left-handed so it couldn't be traced. They were passed to the front, where the teacher leafed through them almost casually. She stopped at one about halfway down the pile, stiffened, and left the room. Everyone looked at Balls. "I didn't say nothin' bad. I said she was a good teacher." Huebrick walked back, her short, blunt heels hard, determined.

"I'm going to read this to you," she said, shaking one of the completed forms, "so you can see just how cruel you are. 'Huebrick ain't got no man and it don't surprise me none. She flat in front and back and fat at the sides. Got hair on her face like a man and her clothes is mammy made.' See that! See!" And she turned the front of the paper toward us, holding it at arm's length with both hands and arced it around the room like a searchlight. "What kind of person would write a thing like that? Tell me!" Everyone was embarrassed, even Balls, as though some important rule had been broken. Sarah stood up in the back of the room, quiet old Sarah who stared at her feet all through school. "I wrote it and I ain't sorry. You wants to know what I think 'bout you and your class, well that's what I think." Miss Huebrick was taken completely off-guard. She had wanted to embarrass us all; maybe she even blamed us all. Clearly she hadn't expected a confession, and when she got one, she didn't know what to do with it. She put Sarah's form down on the desk, leaning for a moment on the paper as she did. The insult once given a person and not just a form caught her again with perhaps greater force. "See me after class, Sarah." We sang "Flow Gently, Sweet Afton" as softly as a children's choir and at the bell filed out. Sarah was in her seat staring, not at her shoes but straight ahead, somehow in her mind, at least, a step ahead of the moment.

Nothing happened to Sarah. The principal was not called in, and she didn't have to take home a note about what she had said. It was generally believed that Huebrick spared Sarah because she was embarrassed to have anyone read the questionnaire. The only thing Sarah would say was that they had a talk. Next class, she was passing out the music books, looking more at home than she ever had. She was one of those students who never asked or answered questions and was so anonymous that teachers never pressed at her. She was present, barely, and stared at the floor, outside even the highly socialized delinquencies of the class. Thin, dark, with untended, ashen skin, she hung out somewhere past the edges of things, at least until Huebrick passed around her questionnaire. There must have been more to the music teacher than any of us guessed. Plainly, she had managed the mire of insult in Sarah's responses enough to know that the questionnaire had not only broken the rules Sarah had tacitly agreed on with the school but that it had teased her into an exchange she could not easily escape. Huebrick must have expected—even reheased a response to— the stylized aggression she regularly got from Balls and the rest of us, in its own way impersonal, aimed more at the situation than at the individual, a feint against the acceptance of order that delighted in theatrical dissarray and the poetic dishevelment of authority. Something in that questionnaire perforated Sarah's isolation. I left the room thinking that Sarah would hit her. Instead, they made friends with each other. It was undoubtedly Sarah's first, and she was fiercely loyal.

One afternoon when Huebrick was out of the room Sarah went to the storage closet, the stockroom of the abandoned retail store—and found Phillip humping a mannequin. She walked back into the room and like a carnival barker shouted, "Wanna see a fool fuck a dummy?" Everyone rushed to the storeroom door. Phillip scrambled to get himself together, catching his shirttail in the hinge that joined the mannequin's leg and hip. Sarah went to the door to keep Miss Huebrick from having to see any of it. Phillip tore his shirt to the waist, then had to push and swing his way out the door.

"How was it, man?"

"Shut your mouth?"

"Damn straight, man. Shut my book too . . . and you stop lookin' at my inkwell that way."

"Don't you touch my chair, man. This here's a good chair, not one a them whore chairs you go round with."

"You all stop that now. Can't you see you's embarrassin' old

Phillip." Phillip was taut and immobile in his seat. Balls danced up behind him. "How'd you feel if you had a girl tore your shirt like that?"

Sarah stopped Miss Huebrick beside the empty store windows in the hall. "This the right book, Miss Huebrick?" Things settled down. Phillip hunched into his seat. We sang "Go Down, Moses," "Flow Gently, Sweet Afton," and "As the Caissons Go Rolling Along." Phillip had been as much an outsider as Sarah. He pushed at the school now and then, mimicking Ball's flicking cool, and always, somehow, failing. He had sucked his thumb clear through grade school. Beginning in the fourth grade he wore a leather pouch over his thumb; tied to his hand with leather thongs, it looked like a falconer's hood. In a world where jive was the center of most talk and gesture always began with exaggerated Sugar Ray jostlings, Phillip had no credibility and, therefore, no place. After the mannequin episode, he became everyone's joke. Balls scribbled hair around the inkwell in Phillip's home-room desk, then gestured at it wildly whenever the teacher turned her back. Someone wrote a note to the wood-shop teacher, suggesting that Philip be kept away from the wood pile and the scrap bin and that it would be dangerous to let him use the drill. Otis referred to the cut pieces of plank at Phillip's workbench as "miss." "Excuse me, miss," he would say, bowing as he passed.

Phillip fought back randomly, occasionally flailing out at a taunt, but there was no real reward in any of it. Reuben backed down from a fight with him in the locker room, saying later that he "wouldn't fight no dummy-lover, no matter what." James lost a fight to him but came out ahead when Balls explained it away as a jealous rage that began when James leaned against Phillip's favorite tree. Phillip shouted at Balls awhile, then slipped away, disappearing almost completely from view.

the red menace

It was Gerald, who was himself called Red Fox, who first called Russell the Red Menace.

"Don't nobody fuck with Russell; he's the Red Menace."

"Damn right, and if you fuckers don't watch out, I'm gonna overthrow this whole country by force of arms." Impressive flex of his long, brown arms—that brown which is romantically called bronze, mythically called red, the penny-brown of the Sioux. "Then, I'm gonna scalp your black ass."

"You ain't gonna scalp shit. The cavalry'll ride all over you, just like always."

"Man, what you think the cavalry's gonna be doin' at your house?"

"Waitin' on his mama."

"On *your* mama, that line gonna be so long, come all the way round the corner and down the street."

"We ain't got no worries about the cavalry this time, man, 'cause we got the Atomic bomb."

"Shee-it."

"That's right—stole it last week."

"You ain't stole nothin'."

"You remember that test last week, the one they canceled on account a the weather."

"Yeah."

"Well, there weren't no weather. We stole it . . . right off that fuckin' tower."

"Bull . . . shit. Ain't nobody can steal an Atomic bomb. They got guards all over that desert."

"Sure they do, but we got Apaches and an Apache can sneak up on anybody and steal anything."

"Man, I ain't never heard such shit in all my life. What they do with it?"

"First, the Apaches caught them slouch-ass soldiers off-guard and cut their fuckin' throats, then they took that bomb right off that damn tower and carried it off."

"Where to?"

"To their secret camp, dumbass. Don't you know that whole desert is in Apache country. Man, they know every inch of it, and ain't nobody but another Apache can follow their trail either."

"What if the army's got scouts?"

"Yeah, Kit Carson."

"Would you get serious. Kit Carson died a hundred years ago; there ain't no more scouts. All those fuckers know how to do now is drive jeeps."

"Yeah, well how many Apaches know how to use an Atomic bomb? Just a bunch a dumb-ass Indians sellin' blankets and moccasins."

"We ain't got no trouble workin' the bomb. We're the Red Menace, man, we got all those Russian spies workin' for us, and they sure as hell know how to work a bomb."

It all made sense. Out in the desert the Apaches, bareback riding their spotted ponies, and on a travois skidding through the sand, an Atomic bomb, Indian women behind them brushing the trail clean with branches, two Russians in over-sized overcoats—even in the roasting New Mexico sun—riding on a buckboard beside them. They enter the box canyon; an Indian on a high, painted desert cliff waves them in with a carbine. There was another sense to it as well, one that came later. When Senator Joseph McCarthy was censured in the Senate, patriotic Omahans gathered petitions to support him against his colleagues. They collected them in a log cabin—the same log cabin that was used each summer to sell rodeo tickets. Perhaps the Red Menace in some corner of the collective patriotic unconscious was red Indian after all, and the "enemy within" that oldest of American enemies.

Russell was an Omaha Indian, great-grandson of Logan Fontenelle, last chief of the Omahas, whose name was given to the housing project where we all lived presumably because he had given up all his people's lands without a fight, saying, perhaps, "Better Red than dead." Logan Fontenelle—fellow traveler, dupe, highly trained, paid subversive, card-carrying member of the Yankee conspiracy, what they called in school *a dignified statesman*, a credit to his race, or a man caught with impossible alternatives among a domestic people. Russell's family lived on the flood slake of the Missouri out past the dikes long before upriver dams tamed the river, and wintered in the tenements above Bum's Park downtown, usually in the crumbling flats over Canfield's Army Store, where we all bought war surplus canteens, throwing knives, and rucksacks for occasional pioneer excursions into the woods of Fontenelle Forest or Mandan Park on bluffs just south of the city. When we were in grade school Russell had a Palomino horse he once rode in a Halloween parade. He wore shiny cowboy shirts, boots with carved tops, and a Stetson. For a long time Indians dressed like cowboys because they, too, were Westerners, or because that was for so long the next rung up in America, a vantage point for some aspiration. Grade school had a place for Russell, niched out of the comfortable place it gave to Indians in general. There were enough nice little Indian stories, show-and-tell, Cub Scouts—an obvious, if temporary, value attached to his past, and there was that awe-inspiring horse, the tribal bonnet and beadwork shirt he once wore. He left the school at strange intervals as the borders of the school district played Monopoly with the mud bar where he lived, or as the Board of Education settled ponderously the matter of his family's permanent residence among the other city Indians who lived in the army surplus store's tenement. By junior high school Russell had grown tall and thin and had one of those Indian faces early painters loved—high cheekbones, long, straight nose, strong chin, deep cheeks—the romantic Indian profile of civic statues and the buffalo nickel. He was not especially athletic, was a clumsy baseball player, but Gerald was right, he was very strong and an unbeatable street fighter. His voice had that swallowing thickness Siouan gives to English, slightly operatic in the way it stays in the throat, ironic, and menacing. He had become the school's silent antagonist, stayed home regularly, slept in class. Even when he was awake, he slouched down so deep into his chair that his head would rest on the back and his chest curve under the writing arm. I don't remember his ever being in trouble; he just stayed silent. He quit school as soon as he could, and I saw him only occasionally around town driving a black Pontiac, which in pre-GTO, LeMans, Bonneville days still had an Indian hood ornament jutting out into the traffic, a face that could have been modeled on Russell's. He worked on construction jobs in the summer; in winter he changed tires at the Yellow Cab garage. The last time I saw him I was stopped at a traffic light next to an Omaha construction site. He was slaked over with powdered concrete, carrying a puddler's hoe, close enough for me to call out his name. We talked briefly through the window, determined that we were both fine, both getting by, both married. I was working that summer in a steel mill and was wearing work clothes and a fatigue hat.

"You still in school?"

"Just graduated. I'm working for the summer, then going to school again."

"That's a good thing. Blain went to airline school in Denver. The only airline job he can get is loading suitcases. That your car?"

"Yeah." It was my first foreign car. He clearly disapproved. "What is it?"

"Borgward," I said as the light changed and I drove away.

"Take it easy, man." I was embarrassed by my car, the first gesture of that infidelity I still practice against my simplest crush on the automobile, a feeble snobbery which raises the stakes of that affection and so makes it more acceptable. Russell had known that and had known also that I was *in school*, despite my clothes and the flakes of steel a bending machine had sprayed me with all day. He knew me, knew the parameters of my life as well as I knew his. We had known each other back to the beginnings of both our memories; the alphabet had seated us together through much of grade school and junior high. If we had talked longer, he would have chided me for owning such a silly little car, but would have tolerated the smart-ass gesture of it in the same way he had tolerated all my years of arm-waving eagerness in school. He had always known the stakes of the games I played and the stakes of his own. The ironies of his situation were my business—the concrete he puddled for Peter Kewitt and Company was being pasted over his land, after all, flooring offices up over the city that still carries his people's name in exchange for a Pontiac every few years, pocket money through the cold winter, and visits to the reservation at Macy with nostalgic, ritual moments and blue corn mush. When he dressed up he would have still worn hand-carved boots and pants with a western cut, a shirt with mother-of-pearl snaps and a jacket with a chevroned, ranch-owner's seam across the back—the clothes of the fantastic figure America had daydreamed into myth as his ancestoral friend-enemy. I dressed in Ivy League mixed with Beat in those days—tweed jackets and Oxford-cloth shirts—

disguised as something I would also never be, a don or a junior fellow, studying a slightly shambled appearance that might indicate boredom with generations of wealth and comfort, the signs of a distracted attention about wordly things that went with a love of poetry and art. The only fad in national disguises I have ever fully resisted is the one indulged by the vagrants of the middle class, which puts on work shirts and boots; that's too close to the truth of the class America gave to Russell's people and mine.

The skim of irony I give to Russell is easy enough; I shouldered my own, still do. Russell is not a cowboy. I doubt that it was ever a serious pretense; instead, it's the costume that was left behind when the dust settled in the dream theater of the West. Breechcloths and leggings did not survive into the modern world. Although they signal in many ways his disinheritance, figure forth again the battle his people lost, they are tied, as well to the place where we fantasize the struggle to have occurred. The only fight my college and graduate school gear had to do with was one I fought with myself that had no circled wagons or great battles and whose scufflings required French philosophy and the modern European novel in place of any of the traditional warrior's skills.

Some of the steel I had helped bend that day would be delivered in time to the construction site Russell was working and would be wired into place to reinforce the concrete he puddled, and so, in some strange way, the building would be a collaboration between us—a last joint venture neither of us would ever have any use for, though even that apparent thematic finality has to be modified, since my brother-in-law would later work in that building as a draftsman. Finally, the bargain, however unspoken, was unevenly struck. My brother-in-law is a convenient signal for the general political fact that once completed, the building would devolve to my people and not to Russell's. Among that concrete and steel my sister's husband supported his family drawing out the plans for further developments, more ambitious projects. Perhaps Russell still supports his pouring their lattices of steel full of concrete. It is a symbiosis in which Russell always gets the losing share. Within the design of success America fed us all, my brother-in-law's slightly greater share is thought a victory, and the immense holdings of the construction company that owns it all are called "the way it is."

Against such knowledge one holds out whatever dreams imagination and nightmare make possible. That atomic bomb, not much bigger than a suitcase I'm sure, might still rest in a high cave at the end of a box canyon out in the desert, holding within its sleek titanium and steel hull the secret reserve of energy each of us needs, if only in supposition, some access to, an assertion that gathers, if only in its style or its garmentry, a brief collective momentum, so that for a few moments the fears of a whole country rest with you. This is what Russell held that day, not merely the bomb but the bomb's plausibility balanced among those other fancied plausibilities—the movies, comics, the entire popular flotsam American culture dealing with the West had made for us. What he understood, intuitively, was what all the rhetoricians of apocalypse have always understood—that the signal points of our real fears are lying all about us and that turning them to any purpose is a poetic act of cultural alignments, a fine tuning, conducted through language, of what is already in scrambled view. Finally, the bomb is no more real than the stereotypical movie Apache, the painted desert no more tangible than the hulking Russian agent. There is no measured ontology to the stuff of this culture; there are only levels of energy. In one way or another everything in America is an icon; nothing is merely an object until it is thrown away, literally heaped out there with the garbage at the town dump or just slipped from our attention, waiting to be recovered as either bric-a-brac or nostalgia. In his own turn Russell and his people have been recovered. The

Indian has been regenerated to our view; at a fresh level of *haute culture* he is loved all over again. Russell's classic profile is not yet back on the hood of his Pontiac, but his beadwork swings chicly across the chests of thousands and his language is being ramshackled by hundreds of poets. The territory of his clothes—his tether to the dissolving West—is now fully invaded. He is a charm America once again needs—fringed jackets, slouched western hats, beads, Zuni silver, and, in museums, spirit wheels and ghost shirts.

John, a mixed Otto, Ponca, and Pawnee, who lived in the apartment next to mine for several years, developed a more lasting attraction to the bomb than Russell. In junior high and the first year of high school he was determined to become a nuclear physicist. He read everything he could on atomic power and the bomb, very early on passing his own ability to comprehend what he was reading. His talk was impressive, though, full of technical language. He encanted the names and numbers of radioactive materials, described cyclotrons, and hallowed critical mass as though it were a precise mixture of Christ's return to earth and an orgasm. What John lacked in all this was Russell's poetic perceptiveness. Russell stole the bomb; John presumed that he could acquire it. His real fancy was to build one. In his most unrestrained moments he wished himself the ability to make one immediately, but day to day he was willing to defer that fantasy to years of reading and study. He wanted to grow up to build an atomic bomb. In the meantime he satisfied himself, as so many others of my friends did, with carbon, saltpeter, and sulphur tamped into smoky, black-powder bombs or the white glow of stolen magnesium strips billowing out their chalky smoke above the sidewalk. John and others like him—my second cousin, who in search of the atom burned down his parents' garage and, finally, in high school blew off his best friend's arm at the shoulder—were the true believers, who applied the Christian premise, "Faith without works is dead," to that dream of destructive supremacy. Across the country many of them did, in fact, die, consumed with their own mini-atolls, gerry-made altars of Gilbert Cemistry set remnants and workbench junk set up in basements and garages.

John took the culture at its word and so determined to work at books and school and putter about his chemicals at night. It lasted, this attention to science, about two and a half years, then he grew interested in fighting—not boxing, street fighting—studying with all the enthusiasm he had given to the atom what Russell seemed to have naturally. School had been made more frustrating by his motivation. The aspiration was too high for the results available to him. He wasn't ever especially good in class, but even if he had been, I doubt that it would have helped. He wanted a mushroom cloud and all that went with it. General science offered, at best, stained litmus paper and a pat on the back. Given such a meager reward, he opted for a good right and the sidewalk terror that went with it.

The bomb was to sheer power what a cool million was to wealth, and in one sense every fanciful aspiration to power had as its new ultimacy that cloud in the desert we all desperately loved and feared. Personal strength and a few dollars were both understandable; their acquisition was mundane, idiosyncratically possible or impossible. Obviously, it was easier for any of us to be a bad-ass, though, than for any of us to be economically even solvent. We did not speak of solvency; as a result we spoke of wealth—a million bucks—and television provided Mr. Anthony of *The Millionaire* to give it all some credibility. Science, all that dangerous black-powder tinkering, was the credibility the bomb's figure of overwhelming power required. There was for the bomb, as there was for money, a regular, societal route to be taken—years of school, late nights of study, self-denial in the college laboratory while others drank beer and felt up girls, but I think John and the rest of the self-styled physicists knew what the compromises of that route were. After all that sacrifice, you could probably not be your own sane version of the mad scientist, whose power was all his own. After years of wear, you would be someone else's scientist, building someone else's bomb. That was the clear message of the Oppenheimer case; at such levels in the balance of power, the scientist was not allowed his madness, whatever it was; the bomb was not his to press or restrain. In our world Dr. Frankenstein, however benevolent, worked at someone else's authority. Oppenheimer was the victim of the Red Menace, whose terror his weapons presumably gave us the strength to repel. For a short while John, the punch-out artist, had a power that was all his own. Russell had never been tricked by science or school and had both—the reputation as a bad-ass and out there in the desert, with Russians tricked into playing firewater salesmen and gun runners, had, at least in our imaginings, an atomic bomb as well.

The scientist has always been an equivocal figure in America, perhaps in Western culture generally. Einstein's name came to stand for genius. "He's real brainy, a regular Einstein," and that explosion of white hair, the bulb nose, and large head were parts of American iconography. He represented one of the self-stranding risks of sustained serious thought, a comic figure, who wore sweatshirts and tennis shoes everywhere and was visually related to movie comedians, particularly Harpo Marx. I was often reminded in those days that though Einstein could "figure out all that stuff," he couldn't change a tire or fix a broken toaster. "What do you want to be? Some kind of egghead, a longhair?" Disastrous qualities that were acquired like the hair masturbation would eventually grow on your palm. Another admonition could serve both situations: "You keep that stuff up, kid, and you'll go crazy."

Eventually, the world would require for its salvation a breed of tough, handsome, athletic nuclear physicists, as quick with a theorem as the cowboy was with his gun. With a few more movies and the right opportunities, John could have given the world its first bad-ass scientist and so balanced those two different powers. Adolescent common sense and the movies both seemed to require a moment of personal physical strength and daring, however complex and technical its setting might become. That is, I guess, too baroque a fancy to survive in the movies or youthful imagination. Movie heroes would specialize, just as John did, in strength and daring, years later casting up totally specialized secret agents to save us—specialized and in the cynical mode of the sixties, professionalized. In the climactic scene in *Goldfinger* James Bond stammers over the intricacies of an atomic bomb in Fort Knox as its digital clock ticks off the seconds till oblivion. Having fought his way through a host of villains, including an invincible Oriental, he only has to disarm the whirring mechanism of the bomb. He begins to reach in, then pulls back. At the last second on the clock in the bomb a hand reaches in from behind him and pulls the appropriate switch. Bond was good at overgadgeted weapons and that tricky Aston-Martin they gave him; science had in its more crucial manifestations gone too far. Knight–errantship, however well paid, had found one of its limits.

Like any number of renegade chieftains, Russell had an unerring sense of tactics. ("Don't make the mistake of underestimating Santana, son. He may be a filthy *savage*, but he's a brilliant tactician, the best I've ever met in the field.") He understood the exact point at which the schools no longer found him charming, and understood, implicitly at that point, that the culture as a whole no longer found him charming either. He had passed up his role as Little Beaver and had outgrown the Indian parts in school plays about Thanksgiving. With a lot of other kids—white, black, and red—John presumed that there was magic in achievement, first scientific, then pugilistic. Russell had never given up the essential secrets of himself as an Indian. Tough as he was, his real strength was in mystery. Remembering that mystery and assessing that early, his deep antagonism to the society were crucial to that bomb-stealing vision of his. All the problems of science and technology were solved by the magic of difference—difference and the unities of antagonism. We have come back to the Indian now for his secrets and his blessings. If he is smart, he will give us neither.

don't ask me, i just work here part-time

"There was this guy and he had a little boy and he took his little boy out and the little boy caught cold, see, so he put him in a hole and he got burnt. Just goes to show: keep your little boy in your hand and you'll never go wrong."

That's Whiskey-Nose Louie, dishwasher and moralist behind his dish table, dealing dinner plates into a metal rack.

"Keep your little boy in your hand and you'll never go wrong." He's working it into his Lord,-I-was-a-sinner voice.

"How many times you been saved, Louie?"
"Four hundred, at least. They ain't a Bible thumper from here to Kansas City ain't saved me at least once or twice. . . . Lord, I was a sinner."
"Amen."
"I was a drinker. Yes, Lord, I was a slave to al-kee-hawl."
"Amen."

"And I was a fornicator . . . a fornicator, Lord."

"Amen to that, amen."

"But now I got the way, Lord, I got the way. I got the light. Yes, Lord, I got me the light and Lord, Lord, I got the truth. I got the truth Lord. I got the way. I got the light. I got the truth."

"Yes, Lord."

"I got the way and the truth and the light."

"Amen."

"Now, that there is a five-dollar salvation. For a little extra I throw in my poor old mom and talk 'bout how bad I did the old lady and how she always prayed for me even when I was doin' her bad. For fifteen dollars, I throw a fit, praisin' the Lord."

"Louie, you're gonna be damned for blasphemin'." Old Gramma, the glass washer behind her own counter, a picture-book old lady, who was always just about to leave for Arizona.

"Damned if I do and damned if I don't, old woman. Hey Sonny, you ever hear me speak in tongues?" He rolls his eyes back and starts babbling, Lucite pink tongue bit out against his lips. "The holy spirit got me again. Old woman, you see them tongues a fire-dancin' round my mouth?"

"All I see is a drunken old blasphemer."

He could go on like that for eight hours, rasping out sexual advice, insult, salvation, and could curse longer without repeating himself than anyone I ever knew. "You want a good time, sonny," he'd say, leaning on the stainless steel counter, swaying his shoulders like a hooker, then he'd bend forward. "Here's what you do—get yourself a broom handle and go down to the river. Find yourself a place where the mud's real dark and soft just where the bank comes outa the water, then you poke that broom handle in there so you got a nice hole, then you put your pecker in and go at it. Some a the best stuff in the world!"

"Louie, I ain't gonna stand it no more. You leave that boy alone!"

"Shut up, old woman, this here's a strong lad, there'll be plenty left for you."

It is hard not to hate the people you serve. As the night wore on, the patrons of the Castle Hotel's dining rooms became more and more intolerable—because they were rude or patronizing or because they were simply oblivious to my presence, fouling box after box of dinnerware for me to sort out onto Louie's work table. Louie! Louie was essential. I would look at the customers and think how they would wretch if they saw him and knew that he had washed the forks they were putting in their mouths. *Excuse me, ladies and gentlemen. I want to take just a minute to introduce our dishwasher, Whiskey-Nose Louie.* It was a cruel fantasy, I suppose, one I harbored for three years. Louie would push through the swinging doors from the kitchen, dressed in his favorite costume—garbage-stained chartreuse pants, their wide, Palm Beach cuffs soaked with dishwater, his Ringling Brothers and Barnum and Bailey T-shirt, gray hair curling through the holes at the armpits, a wet, gray garbage ground under its faded lion and flaming hoop, yellow golf shoes turned up at the toes, no socks or shoelaces, matted gray hair and permanent three-day beard. His skin was dinged and limp as an old rag, and his nose, his famous nose, looked as though it had been roughly shaped out of old ham-burger. *Say a few words to our guests, Louie. Tell them the difference between hormones and vitamins. "When a whore moans, she must need vitamins."* Then he would be off on one of his rants about prostitutes and their unparalleled virtues. "I never in my life met an honest woman with half the sense of a good whore. That's the truth. Everybody's always complainin' 'bout women doin' 'em wrong, that's 'cause they mess with the wrong class a women. You get yourself a good whore, boy, and do her right." Or he would lecture on health—"You take all these people got back trouble. Know what that comes from? Crooked fuckin', that's what. More'en half the people in this country do it crooked." Or politics—"Eisenhower? Shit, I can tell you 'bout Eisenhower. Used to was he played football, till he got his ass kicked by an Indian named Tharp. What kinda man is that to be a general? That's why they put him in Europe and not the Pacific, cause Eisenhower ain't worth a fart in a high wind, not since that Indian got on him."

Louie lived on Jefferson Square, Omaha's Bums' Park, in the Chicago Hotel, once a city high spot, long since fallen to winos, prostitutes, and wintering Indians. Summer and winter the skewed doors stood half-open wafting a taint of urine and sour milk into the square. He was fired from the Castle kitchen every three or four months—often it seemed calculated—for drinking on the job or swearing out through the dining room doors. He would go off for a while to the kitchen at the Hill or the Rome. Then one day he'd be back at his old stand. And he always managed to get back in without having to pretend a complete conversion to one of the hostesses. The appalling contritions required of Bill, Louie's wino helper, and Old Man Charlie, the night man, were avoided by simply turning up in an apron and going to work.

Once a coffee shop hostess tried to save Louie and the kitchen in general by hiring a Grace Bible Institute student and putting him on Louie's shift. The poor fellow lasted less than a day. His name was Arnold, and he looked like a farm-hand on his first day out as a magazine salesman, scrubbed up and slicked down with oversized but still tentative gestures, hopelessly eager. It was like throwing a wet tea bag into an electric fan. Louie called him *Hank*. "My name's Arnold."

"Sure, Hank."

"Arnold, Arnold!"

"Whatever you say, Hank."

As the work got harder, the steam around the dishwashing machine heavier, the din of plates from bus trays dumped out on the stand unceasing, Louie continued to address him as Hank. Poor Arnold, he could only get an answer to a question about the job when he stopped insisting on Arnold and gave in to Hank. The whole kitchen set on him. Leo, the first cook, began throwing mashed-potato balls at his head or at his piles of clean plates. "You leave my boy Hank alone, Leo." By midday Arnold had disappeared entirely into Hank. The hostess came out to see how he was getting along.

"How are things going, Arnold."

"His name's Hank."

"Oh, I thought it was Arnold."

"Naw, it's Hank, ma'am. Ain't that true, boy."

"Yes, sir," he said, staring into a silverware rack.

"Old Hank here was just tellin' me how they jerk off in unison out there at that Bible school. You tell her about it, Hank. . . . Come on back, ma'am, it's real interestin'. They got this conductor like, and he stands up in front just wavin' his pecker and Hank and all the boys follow right along. You tell her, Hank." Arnold ran out behind the hostess and was never seen again. She came back after the rush was over and told Louie that he was a cruel man and that Arnold had just broken down and cried in the lobby. "Just goes to show," said Louie, "all that jerkin' off can take the spine right out of a man. I was you, I wouldn't hire anymore a them Bible school boys."

One night when Louie was going on about the evils of politicians ("Jerkoffs," he said, "biggest bunch of jerkoffs I know. I ever tell you about Eisenhower and that Indian?"), I told him that I was going to be a Communist. He was outraged. It was as though he had wasted all his teachings on me. I was the hopeless student who had completely missed the point of everything he had ever told me in noisy confidence across the dish table.

"A Communist, you must be crazy! Why a Communist ain't no better than a queer. Worse. At least a queer'll buy you a drink. A Communist'll talk at you like a preacher, . . . 'cept Communists won't shut up till you agree with them. And you don't even get a bowl a soup."

"Louie, you don't know nothin' 'bout Communists."

"Don't know, don't know. Why shit, I been shouted at by

Communists from here to San Francisco and back again. No sooner they get outa Communist school than they look me up. Sometimes I go out the back door just to keep from steppin' on them."

"Bull."

"Comes with bein' a deegenerate. They hunt you down—preachers, social workers, democrats, missionaries, Communists—all of 'em. And outa the whole bunch, the worst is a Communist."

"'Cause they won't buy you a drink?"

"You ever see the women that go around with Communists? Ugly and fat, every damned one of them, big fat arms, legs like pool tables. That's 'cause they hate good-lookin' women, just hate 'em."

"Louie, that doesn't make any sense."

"Course it doesn't. If they made any sense, they wouldn't be Communists. You meet a Communist, you ask 'em what he thinks about good-lookin' women, then look out, cause you're gonna get a two-hour speech about capitalism and jewelry and widows with nine kids hitched up to plows and bankers and how a poor woman suffers for every jewel a fancy woman wears. All the while, he's got some quarter section a beef in a brown dress sittin' in the corner bitin' her fingernails. Never trust a man who's got a smart reason for havin' somethin' he don't want. Nother thing, they call you *comrade*. How'd you like to be called comrade by some jerkoff in a Salvation Army overcoat? Or worker? Huh? You want to be called a worker? Then after they get done insultin' you, they start up tellin' you how it's all somebody else's fault that you got so fucked up. I was in Portland one night, in a freightyard, not botherin' nobody, drinkin' Seattle wine with this here gandy-dancer. And up come this Communist. Spends half-a-minute talkin' 'bout the weather, then gets goin' on the capitalists and how they put us all outa work, and I says to him, 'Where's your fat girlfriend?' And he says he ain't got a fat girlfriend, and I tells him that the Communists fucked him straight cause he's entitled to a fat girlfriend. Then me and that gandy-dancer bust a gut laughin'. And he asks what's so funny, and I says, 'They're s'posed to give you a fat girlfriend. It goes with bein' a Communist. And he says he ain't no Communist, he's a socialist worker. And I says, long as you're gonna be somethin' dumb, might as well be a Communist, cause a fat, ugly woman is better than no woman at all."

Grandma is furious. "Louie, you got a big mouth and no sense. You boys listen to me. The Communists ain't no joke. Them Russians want to take over everything and rule the world. They got spies everywhere, even in the Army."

"Old woman, you really believe all that shit?"

"It's the truth."

"Truth? What you know about the truth? Dried up old woman!"

"The Russians want to take over everything, right?"

"So do I. That don't make me no Communist."

"And that Joe Stalin. He's the head Communist and . . . "

"Stalin ain't no Communist!"

"What?"

"Can't you hear either? How you get the idea Stalin's a Communist?"

"How'd I get the idea? Everybody know he's a Communist, the head Communist."

"Woman, you're too dumb to be loose on the streets. Stalin ain't no Communist. Stalin's a tricker."

"A tricker?"

"That's right. He tricked Hitler and he tricked Roosevelt and he tricked Churchill and he tricked Harry Truman. One a the best trickers in the world, and a tricker ain't a Communist. Never was a Communist tricker and they ain't never gonna be one."

"Stalin is the head of Russia and Russia is a Communist country. Right?"

"Damn right, and that's one a the best tricks of all. You want a worry about somethin', old woman, you worry about when

Stalin dies, cause soon as he does that whole big country's gonna be run by Communists. Then we'll all be in trouble."

"Louie, Stalin's already dead. He died last year."

"Huh?"

"He died last year."

"Leo! Did Stalin die last year?" Leo nods. "Jesus! Stalin dead. Don't surprise me they tried to keep it a secret."

"What about the Chinese?" Grandma, again.

"What about 'em?"

"The Chinese Communists?"

"Woman, you believe everything you hear? They ain't no Chinese Communists. I bet you met a man on the street wearin' a rubber raincoat told you he was a balloon you'd try to blow him up. Chinese is Chinese, smartest damned people in the whole world, kicked out that guy that wanted to be like Stalin, Chang Ki-Check, that lives on that island, what's its name?"

"Formosa."

"That's it. Old Chang Ki-Check thought he was a tricker, but he wasn't half good enough for trickin' a Chinaman, and they kicked him out. Then we take up with him, 'cause there ain't nothin' American politicians is closer to than a half-ass tricker. That's the reason the Chinese started up in Korea. If we let 'em have old Chang, like we shoulda, there wouldn't a been no Korean War in the first place. I ever tell you 'bout Chinese women, kid?"

"Yes, you did, Louie."

"When I was in Seattle I lived two years with this Chinese whore. Name was Mabel, but I always called her Fong Yu. Made me that scarf of mine, the one with the big "L" on it. Best woman I ever knew. Don't try to tell me about Chinamen, 'cause I know."

"If she was such a good woman, why'd you leave her?"

"I didn't leave her. She left me. Woke up one mornin' and said to me, 'Louie, I'm too old for whorin' and too smart to stay with an old drunk like you.' Then she just packed up and left. Two a the best years a my life was spent with old Mabel. 'Fong

Yu,' I'd say. 'Fong yerself,' she'd say right back. I ever show you the scarf she made me?"

Mabel's scarf was made from a long strip of pink baby blanket with fringes from an even older scarf stitched to the ends. There was a slit cut in the middle, lengthwise, roughly hemmed to keep it from fraying. At one end there was a large, swirling "L" embroidered in darning thread. Louie would adjust the scarf around his neck, then pull the monogrammed end through the slit, fluffing it out so the "L" would show and carefully tucking the sides under the lapels of his gray overcoat.

In his own way, Louie had style—those Palm Beach pants, the circus T-shirt, golf shoes, Mabel's scarf, his sweat-stained fedora, the relentless wisdom and reveling vulgarity, all of it fit together like an invention. He was unique in the kitchen because his pretense was all aimed at what, in fact, he was, an old skid-row drunk, and it gave him an immense advantage over everyone else. The rest of them all had ways out, tenaciously held delusions wired to another job, a former life, distant relatives, anything outside the kitchen, chanted like round dances night after night.

"I don't need this shit job. I got plenty a people would take me on just like that. You know that bastard come in here again, think I'm good shit, gonna jump up and down for him, he's got another think comin', that's what I say. I got this kid in California been askin' me to come out there and live with him, got a beautiful place out there, sun shines all the time, not any a this shit weather we got around here. I can go any time I want to, that kid writes six seven times a month sayin', 'Dad, why don't you come out here and live with us,' but I figure I'll go back to the draglines first, six thirty-five an hour, union scale. Can do that any time I fuckin' A want to, and that bastard thinks he can push me around like that again he's gonna find out." This is Bill, Louie's partner behind the dishstand, a wino with a banker's face—long, oval and symmetrically creased at the sides of his mouth, an even fringe of gray hair edging a freckled bald head, round wire-rimmed glasses. His insistence that he could leave anytime and take up a better life moved around the kitchen like an incantation. Sammy, the night potwasher, was staying just long enough to put together a stake to take him back to Las Vegas. The salad man, Ray, had a deal to go partners in a catering service. Walter and Arnie, two homosexual busboys—one swish, the other butch—both claimed lovers who would take them away to cashmere apartments out West. Every night they clawed at each other's fantasies. Grandma had a daughter in Arizona.

"Ain't nothin' in Arizona 'cept sand dunes, Communists, and morphadites," Louie said. "You go on out to Arizona and the Communists'll get you sure, take you off to one a them sand dunes and turn you into a morphadite."

"I ain't even listenin' to you, you old drunk."

"Probably got your daughter already. They'll take 'em old, but they like 'em young. Likely got herself a carnival job right now. Got old Bill's kid in California, and now he's the two-headed boy."

"I seen a two-headed boy in Waterloo, up at the fair."

"When was that?"

"Ten, fifteen years ago."

"Musta been some other two-headed boy. They didn't get Bill's kid till last year sometime. Ain't that right Bill."

"You shut up about my boy."

"Sure thing. Know just how you feel. One a my kids got turned into a two-headed boy I wouldn't want to talk about it either. All I was doin' was trying to save old Grandma here from goin' off to git herself turned into a morphadite."

"You'll be surprised one day when I don't show up 'cause I'm in California. Got a letter from that kid just last week askin' me to come on out there, saying . . . "

"Two heads is better than one."

". . . we got plenty of room."

"That's just what Darlene said in her birthday card."

"You mean she's got two heads, too. Goddamn them commies, if it wasn't enough to make the poor girl a morphadite, they give her two heads to boot."

"Said she could get my room ready in no time at all."

"What they do is they take you out, all tied up, to this sand dune run by these Indians and they make a doll looks just like you, 'cept that it's a morphadite or got two heads or whatever. Then they feed you this cactus juice and do a dance and, zap, quick as anything, you're a two-headed morphadite."

"Stupid old drunk. Ain't no such cactus juice and no Communists in Arizona."

"You said so yerself, old woman, 'The Communists is everywhere.' And that includes Arizona. What you think a Pinko is? Just another word for a morphadite. Wait till them dirty old commie Indians got you out there in the sand feedin' you that atomic cactus."

"What atomic cactus?"

"The cactus they get from that place where they set off the bomb. That's what makes you a morphadite."

Grandma turns back to her dirty glasses, sulking, and Bill pulls a rack of wet dishes out of the dishwashing machine. Walter preens his red pompadour. "I knew a man from Arizona, and he certainly wasn't a morphadite."

"Musta been a Communist or an Indian."

"He was not!"

"Maybe they don't bother with fairies."

"Sooner than they'd bother with an old hag like you."

Louie pats his hand under the gray hair at the back of his neck, tilts his head, and smiles. "Takes one to know one."

Leo bangs a sauce spoon along the bottoms of the pots and pans that hang over his steam table. "Coffee!" an exclamation set somewhere between the cry for water by a man lost in the desert and a master sergeant's command, an authoritative gasp. Paul, the simple-minded, muscle-bound busboy heaves his shoulder into my side, steps back, and yanks his apron up to his chin. "My name's Paul. See my army belt. I was in the Army. Two years. See my army belt. Feel my muscle. Wanna step on my toe." He lifts his bicep like a cartoon strongman, then pushes his foot across my path. "Go on, step on it." Paul bought web belts and jump boots from the army surplus store down the street from the hotel. In that grapple of intelligence that seems always to be going on in the retarded, as though a nimble mind were somehow mired far back, Paul had years before caught hold of the Army, not quite an idea nor anything so complex as a lie, rather something held firmly, frantically, a twig against the enveloping quagmire. For three years he introduced himself. He would walk up from behind and hit me hard in the shoulder. "My name's Paul. I was in the Army. Two years. Wanna hit me back?" He would turn and point at his own shoulder. "Here, go ahead." Or he would stomp the heel of his boot into the toe of my penny loafers, then offer a paratrooper's steel toe in exchange. "I was in the Army. See my army belt? Two years. See?" Or he would hike the apron up at the side and pull out his sweat-contoured wallet. "I got a girl. Wanna see a picture a my girl?" And there, cupped in with his Social Security card, was a senior class picture of a high school girl smiling her yearbook immortality smile, hair ringletted around her face, scalloped Dorothy Collins white collar sharply outlined against her cashmere sweater like a paper cut-out cloud. Everybody knew he had paid Vecchio two dollars for the picture.

"What's her name, Paul?"

"Vicki. Her name's Vicki. Vicki's her name. She's pretty, huh?"

"Does she do it for you?"

"What? Oh. No, no. She ain't that kinda girl. No. You think she'd do that, huh? That what you think."

"Naw, Paul, she don't look like that kinda girl."

"You say anything like that about my girl, I'm gonna fix you good."

"I didn't say nothin', Paul, nothin'."

"I was in the Army. Two years. See my army belt. Feel my muscle. Go ahead. Hit me. You wanna hit me?"

"No Paul, I don't want to hit you."

"Go on, hit him." Frank, the Marlon Brando-replica busboy who had bit one side of his upper lip until it dented his smile to match Brando's in *The Wild One*. "Come over here and step on my toe, half-wit, and I'll put this boot down your throat," he shouts, one pant leg raised to expose a biker's engineer boot.

"Wanna see a picture of my girl, Frankie?"

"Sure, Paul."

Paul takes the photograph from his wallet and stretches it out to Frank's hand, a peace offering of sorts. Frank puts it in his palm, looks at it admiringly a moment, then pushes it face first into his crotch, tugging out at a handful of apron and starched linen fly, swaying and moaning, "Oh, Vicki."

"You give it back. Stop that. Give it back."

Paul advances one step, and Frank is up on his toes, left hand jabbing out at Paul's face, right circling. "You gonna step on my toe, Army man?" The picture drifts to the floor like a falling leaf. Paul stoops to recover it, and Frank's boot booms to the kitchen tile half an inch from Paul's fingers. Paul retreats, cowed by the noise and fury of Frank's attack, wiping the picture on his sleeve, staring at Vicki's soiled, smiling face, wiping again, awkwardly meticulous like a caged ape puzzling over a small piece of fruit.

"Bully!"—Walter running to console Paul.

Waitresses in salmon-pink nylon uniforms move in and out of all this like a *corps de ballet*, dodging the goosing point of Leo's sharpening steel and Louie's homespun gynecology.

"Hey, Hilda, what color Cadillac's that man a yours gonna give you?"

"Pink, honey, titty pink," she'd say, hefting an oval tray of sizzling steak platters up to her shoulder. "Titty pink," as her skirt shifted across the taut rubber of her Playtex girdle.

At the back door Washington hunched down over his pot-washing sinks mumbles the names of wines at the soapy tops of baking sheets, a boogy baseline to everyone else's right-hand tirade. "Muscatel. Muscatel. Muss-ahh-tell. Muscatel. Muss-ahh-tell. Muss-ah-ever-tell. Muss-ahh-never-tell. Muss-ahh-never-ever-tell. Muss-ahh-tell. Muscatel." He could talk himself drunk. Well, half-drunk. "You gonna git me some juice tonight, kid?" Orange juice to take the bite off the Sterno he stole from my room service cart and strained through slices of white bread in the locker room.

"Get your own juice, man. I'm the one whose gonna have to pay for that heat if they find out it's gone."

"I don't know nothin' 'bout no heat. I gotta have juice on accounna my sore throat."

"You keep drinkin' that Sterno, man, you gonna have to get a white cane on accounna bein' blind."

"Git me some juice, man, come on."

He would mix the juice and the clear, iridescent liquid in a steam-table pot he would set up on the window ledge behind his pair of steaming sinks and all night long dip out slugs of the mixture with a soup ladle.

"Orange juice. Orange juice. Oh-ran-jews. Oh-ran-jews. Oh-ran-jews."

It went on and on, the whole kitchen like a steam calliope run wild—Leo battering his kettles and flinging mashed potato balls, Mr. C, the sugar-freak glasswasher, flailing with his cane at anyone who spilled water on his glass stand, Paul stomping and punching, Frankie singing "Tutti-Frutti" into a slotted spoon, Walter, president of three local fan clubs, reciting the dimensions of his favorite Hollywood stars and sighing, buxom Hilda deep-breathing toward her pink Cadillac, Blaine playing bongos on a soup kettle, "Day-o, Day-ay-ay-0, Daylight come and me wann go home," Grandma reciting the McCarthy litany on Communism, Bill mumbling on about California, the squawk-box from the dining room calling for glasses, silverware, butter, and ice, Louie speaking in tongues. At the end of a dinner rush your ears would ring with it. It gathered with the steam that made the starched white uniforms go limp, glazed over fingers with hours of garbage until they stiffened and cracked. The hotel bucked overhead. Weekending cattle buyers, 4-H families in for the livestock show, ballplayers, rodeo cowboys, wrestlers, handicappers, Air Force officers flying our five stately call girls to the worn elegance of "modern" rooms, Verne Gange, Yukon Ike, Primo Carnero, the mad bull of the Pampas, Gorgeous George, Johnny Keane, and once even Gene Autry—all seemed like unsteady riders on a shaky carnival ride. While I was there, school, the rest of my life, my family, were stalled out past the parking lot in a night that was always startling for its quiet spaciousness. Even now the edges of it are strange, the ordinary late railroad durability of the hotel remained as dwarfed by the kitchen as it was the first night I worked there. Fragments of nickel-plate, art deco ornaments, and somber lobby furniture, dim corridors, the basement brine tank edged with callus-colored crystals, Hotel Discontinuous—so many drifted pieces, as though it had foundered on a slow wave, leaving to memory only an area of familiar flotsam. The kitchen is intact, though, with Louie at the center overhung with steam, his gray stubble, dishwater-puckered index finger waving in my face, "Wanna have a good time, sonny?"

thump, bam

"Quiet!"

Everyone looked up and muttered.

"I said quiet."

The long-faced librarian with manila hair paced down the broad aisle of the library slapping a yellow ruler into her palm. Mutterings rippled through the rows of long tables, eddied, and curled back.

"Quiet!"

It was as though she were tossing pebbles in a pond. With each command, ponytails and ducktails flashed, faces turned her way, then settled back. Behind her the brass fittings on the card catalog shined like medals on a varnished uniform, and, in the alcove beyond, the books seemed content with their boredom and ours. The library was a study hall. Every seat was assigned, each table charted on a great card the librarian carried down the aisle at the beginning of the hour. If you wanted to go into the stacks for a book, you had to ask permission and were given a pass, which was reclaimed when you checked out your book. If you wanted to use one of the dictionaries along the wall, you had to raise your hand. There were encyclopedias and atlases under the windows and on an ash-blond case near the west door, tightly sealed in a glass cube, there was a scale model of the Taj Mahal made entirely of sugar cubes, the gift of some long departed alumni, a remnant of a more painstaking age. Inside the case, beside the reflecting pond mirror, a card memorialized the sugar cube craftsman and noted the number of cubes used in the dazzlingly white structure. The librarian paused at the case, as though taking her strength from its sweet diligence, then turned back up the aisle.

"Quiet!"

Past the Taj Mahal, through the west doors of the main library, there was a second large reading room called West Library. As hateful as Main Library was, West Library was worse. There were no books and no book alcoves to steal off into, and it was presided over by a fascist Spaniard who wacked talkers over the head with the sharp edge of his ruler. East Library, really an extension of the cafeteria, was ruled by coaches and shop teachers. There were no books, no dictionaries, and no librarians. It was the special ground of athletes and aging shop students, lumbering giants in their early twenties, waiting to go off to their shop-related afternoon jobs. The girls in East Library seemed to come exclusively from the flood-washed flats of East Omaha. They wore Wellington half-boots and tight, boy-cut, V-neck sweaters. They studied retail arts and food services and were picked up outside school each afternoon by tattooed dropouts. My favorite was named Myrtel, a short blonde who carried her ample chest like a recently awarded prize. When she caught me looking her way, she would say, "Fuck off, peach-fuzz" or "Eat it, baby face." Once, when I was talking to an uptown girl in the fourth-floor hall, Myrtel came up and said to the girl, "Watch out, honey, he ain't as sweet as he looks." I liked East Library, but it was a little frightening. It was as though the school had seen through all my academic and social masquerades and sent me back to a staging area for dropouts where I belonged. At mid term I was transferred to Main Library.

"Shit, man, you don't know nothin' about street fightin'. You come down to Hanscom Park, you come down to the South Side, and you'll see."

"Man, I been to Hanscom Park, and all I seen was trees."

"You just say when you want to come."

"I'll come down there the day after you come to 24th and Clark Street."

"I ain't interested in no 24th and Clark Street."

"I know you ain't. You ever been on north 24th Street, man?"

"I ain't never wanted to go there, but . . . "

"Talk on, talk on."

"What you mean?"

"I just said talk on, man, talk on."

"I ain't afraid a no jig–town man. You sayin' I am?"

"Talk on."

"*No talking.*" The librarian turns our way, and voices murmur all around us.

"Anyway, these guys jump on this truck, see, and this one guy's got this weight like on the end of a strap, and he thumps this other guy on the back of the neck, and the weight swings over and hits him right between the eyes . . . the coolest thing you ever seen, and all the time they're playin' "Rock Around the Clock" real loud. And later this guy throws a baseball right at the teacher's head so hard it cracks the blackboard, and this colored guy hits this other guy in the gut, I mean really hard, and the other guy goes 'oooff,' and I mean he just slides down the wall onto the floor. You gotta see it, man. Like this one guy pulls a knife and he's like dancin' around, and they call the teacher—that's Glenn Ford—they call him 'teach' . . . they say 'hey teach.' "

"QUIET! NO TALKING OVER THERE!"

"Anyway, I'm gonna make one a them things with the strap

and the weight. Thump. . . Bam . . . just like that. My buddies and me we're gonna see it again on Friday. Maybe it was leather strings, like for boots, that was tied to the weight. You gotta see it, man. The coolest thing I ever saw."

"QUIET."

"And there's this lady teacher, and she's got the hots for Glenn Ford, see, and she wears real tight skirts and blouses with the collar up and the neck open clear to her tits, and this one guy stays after school and gets her in the library, you know, and she comes out a there with her blouse torn almost off. Like, I mean, she was raped man, right in that movie. You gotta see it."

"WHAT'S YOUR NAME?"

"You talkin' to me, teach?"

"THAT'S RIGHT. WHAT'S YOUR NAME?"

"I ain't done nothin'."

"WHAT'S YOUR NAME?"

"What you want my name for?"

"ALL RIGHT, COME WITH ME."

"One two three o'clock four o'clock rock, five six seven o'clock eight o'clock rock, nine ten eleven o'clock twelve o'clock rock. We're gonna rock, around, the clock, tonight."

Alvin sang it loud, just like Bill Haley and the Comets, all the way to the checkout desk and into the hall. We could hear it echo down the stairs until the steel and safety-wired glass door closed behind him. He was, almost desperately, a teenager. Most of the rest of us just happened to be teenaged. *Blackboard Jungle* became his model; it gave him a way of dealing with himself and with school. He saw the movie over and over again and, finally, did make that weapon out of leather thongs and a chunk of iron, though every time he offered a menacing display of its use, the weight would swing around and hit him on the elbow. He could get it to swing on a long arc by extending his arm, but when he tried to stop his fist at the base of an imaginary neck, the weight would accelerate on the shorter radius of the thongs alone and *thunk*, hit him right in the elbow, then he would curse and stamp and throw the thing on the ground. He finally figured that he needed something like a head to practice on and one day took three of us out onto the track to show how much damage he could do to the stump of a lamppost near the bleachers. We stood back, and Alvin held the thongs, David and Goliath fashion, next to one leg, swinging it gently at first to get the long arc going, then *whoosh*, he swung the whole thing up over his shoulder, smashing his fist into the pole. The iron weight sped over the pole's top and hit the other side a lethal but glancing blow. It ricocheted and hit Alvin in the right cheek. He reeled around, cursing, the leather thongs still knotted in his fist. We helped him back into the school building, and I told the nurse that he was going out for a pass and ran into the goal post. She looked at the ballooning red welt on his face and had him taken to the hospital.

Alvin came back to school the next day brandishing a broken cheekbone and a fantastic black eye. He avoided me and the others who had been there. To anyone else who asked about his injury he said, "I got hit," in a way that suggested an incredible fight, a perfect B-movie intonation, like a phrase thrown over his shoulder to a sidekick also pinned down in a box canyon— *just a flesh wound*, he said, somewhat painfully moving his six-gun to his left hand.

"Man, you see what they did to Alvin?"

"What *they*? He hit himself in the face with that thing he's always swingin' around."

"A bunch a guys from the South Side caught him in an alley."

"Don't you listen. He hit himself in the face with that iron thing of his. I was there."

"What was you doin' on the South Side?"

"It wasn't on the South Side; it was on the track."

"Look, Butera and Caniglia was both there. They jumped in and saved him. You go over there and look at Butera's hand." Butera was on the other side of the hallway, holding his right hand out, knuckles up, for a group of admirers. "It's all cut up, man. I just saw it."

"I don't give a shit about Butera's hand. Alvin hit himself in the face tryin' to get that stupid thing of his to work on that cut-off post out on the track."

"Why don't you go over there to Butera and tell him his hand ain't all cut up and that he and Caniglia didn't jump in and save Alvin's ass from eight or ten guys in an alley on the South Side."

"I ain't got nothin' to say to Butera."

"I didn't think you did."

"But Alvin's a damned liar if he said he was in a fight with anybody cause I saw him thump himself with that iron thing of his. I ain't got nothin' to talk to Butera about, and I ain't interested in his cut-up hand. The way he goes around hittin' stop signs and trees and brick walls, his hand's probably cut up all the time."

"Well, you come over there and tell him he wasn't in a fight yesterday on the South Side savin' Alvin's ass and he'll cut it up some on you."

So Alvin became a hero of sorts and generally respected as an all-around bad-ass. He called people up at night and asked if they wanted to fight. He swaggered around in Big D denims, the South Side uniform, and hung out with Butera and Caniglia. He parted his pompadour in the middle to make two wet, forked curls on his forehead. The *Blackboard Jungle* device disappeared completely. A few months later in the shower after gym class he bumped into Gerald, who was called Red Fox, then told Gerald to watch where he was going. Gerald called him a peckerwood. Alvin raised his fists, but before he could finish his first roundhouse swing, Gerald had hit him ten or fifteen times, Sugar Ray fashion, short, quick jabs flicked out at arm's length, and Alvin the Terrible lay wet and naked on the shower floor, his head cut open from the fall, blood swirling down the drain in a torrent of soapy water. He said later that he had been pushed from behind and that he would "get that nigger." Gerald was completely unperturbed.

Gerald's size should have finished Alvin's reputation, but it didn't. Butera and company were happy to accept Alvin's story about having been pushed and were reconfirmed in their general superstitions about fighting with blacks. At worst, Alvin was considered foolish for having crossed the color line to have a fight, and there was no attempt to get anyone. Alvin had been *oofed* down the shower wall by a tall, skinny, reddish-brown version of Sidney Poitier. What else could he expect? In his own bumbling way he always suceeded through his failures in becoming exactly what he wanted to become—a forgettable third ruffian in a movie that was essentially about someone else. He and his friends—surprisingly, I suppose—would stay on to graduate in woodworking or machine shop, growing abruptly serious, sometimes even tearful, at graduation, signing yearbooks and passing out autographed, billfold-sized portraits of themselves. After a good drunk and a senior picnic brawl, they all joined the Marines in search of bit parts in yet another movie.

Unless he was diverted somehow along the way, Alvin returned from the Marines with enough money for a down payment on his first new car, a Chevy V-8, which he kept clean and polished for one summer's worth of cruising the old drive-ins, then married and settled into the job his car payments had chosen for him. During the 1972 primary campaign George Wallace held a rally in Omaha which got national television coverage because a small group of anti-war hecklers were attacked by Wallace's hard-hat supporters and had to be rescued by the police. As I watched the newsclip, I thought of Alvin and his friends, by then probable Wallacites—angry at welfare, fearful of the blacks, despising the long-haired hippie creeps whose leaders had already cannonized Alvin's brand of 1950's rowdiness as the first stirrings of the revolution. Still, there, I am certain, was Alvin, cheering George Wallace, allied with those old trade unionists who had been my father's friends when they all supported Henry Wallace for president with equal fervor. And if he caught up with a hippie in the fray, well, pity the poor hippie. Alvin had once majored in beating people up. The fact that he was never particularly good at it undoubtedly just added to the fury with which he flailed at this latter-day version of himself.

Alvin and his gang were not really delinquents, though to an outsider they might have seemed frightening enough. The real delinquents were in and out of school very quickly. Many of them left for reform school mid-year; others slouched through East Library until they were sixteen and old enough to drop out. They returned to the afternoon rush on Cummings Street in sagging Buick Dynaflows to pick up girls. I had known most of these hard cases since grade school. One, Harlowe Brown, had promised to kill me in the fifth grade. "What for?" I asked him. "'Cause I hate your guts." He lived in white East Omaha, the small hook of Iowa silt and sand the Missouri had left stranded in Nebraska. He never had much to do with school but spent most of his time around skid row, where he worked nights rolling drunks. During a short stay in the county jail he made a deal with two Kentucky bank robbers awaiting extradition and smashed a guard over the head with a mop handle to help the two escape, only to discover that he was locked in a passageway with the guard he had hit, nowhere near the keys to the cell holding the bank robbers. Eventually he was convicted of manslaughter after the death of an airman outside an East Omaha tavern.

Harlowe was big and puffy with reddish hair greased back into five-inch ducktails below a Vaselined flattop crew cut. He wore wide-legged denims and engineer boots and striped shirts in deep flesh colors with knit waistbands and cuffs. He wore his collars up at the back, and they frayed at the tip of his ducktail until it began to fall in stiff locks around his ears. I saw him at the roller rink occasionally, huffing his way through a crowd of skaters, and at the city's first big rock-and-roll concert, he was the first in the aisle, doing the dirty boogie as he flicked a white handkerchief over his head like a whip.

Brown was widely known as a street fighter, and he decided on the basis of his perfect record in skid-row alleys to enter the Golden Gloves. It was a disaster. He was entered for a three-round preliminary bout as a heavyweight. He bounced into the ring with a roll of pink fat edging the top of his satin trunks. He waved to his fans, tugged mock-professionally at the ropes in his corner, and lumbered out into the center of the ring to pulverize his opponent, a trim, well-trained, serious fighter, who approached Harlowe with a stance taken directly from a gymnasium poster. Harlowe was dancing, gloves bouncing up from his waist, a modified dirty boogie. The boxer had a clear shot at Brown's face with his left lead. He was working on a three-count—three jabs followed by a half-step retreat, bob, half-step return, and three more jabs. It looked as though he'd been fighting Harlowe all his life. With the third jab Harlowe's flailing gloves were up, closing in on the empty space the boxer had just stepped out of, bob, half-step, and return. Within seconds Harlowe's face was bright red and his ducktails were standing straight out to the sides. He looked like a circus clown, and the crowd gave him a clown's reward. By the end of the first round Harlowe was running from his opponent. At the bell he threw up his hands and climbed out of the ring. It was a clear victory for skill and training, but it would have been a mistake for anyone to suppose that his defeat made him any less dangerous on a street or in an alley. Harlowe had a reserve of pure malice that the ring restricted. His strength, which was altogether real and terrifying, was not susceptible to order and form. Most fights are decided, as my father once said, by the eagerness of the participants to quit. Boxing matches have to do with confining the will to win to specific limits of skill and form. Harlowe had no sense of limits of any kind and no interest in form. He would have made as bad a soldier as a boxer. When he settled into crime, he was a bad criminal. I was told by a mutual friend that when he rolled his skid-row drunks he would pose as a police detective. He would ask for the drunk's wallet, take all the cash, and hand the wallet back; then, gratuitously, he would beat the drunk around for a while. Whatever schemes he devised, they seemed always to give way to a simple, impatient love of violence. He must have had something in mind the day he clubbed the jailhouse guard, if not a plan, at least a notion of how it might all come out, but whatever it was, it didn't survive his urge to hit the guard. The small change he got from winos and drunks was more than likely the excuse for the beatings, not the reason for them.

Alvin and his tough-guy friends never intended to be Harlowes. Delinquency, as Alvin perceived it from the movies, required a limited commitment. It was a matter of style, not an obsession or a way of life. It was a disguise, one of many—the Brando disguise, the James Dean disguise, the Joe College disguise—the culture offered and certified, a costume he would eventually shed. Alvin did get into gang fights and thump away at people, who were injured, sometimes even killed, but he always intended for himself that V-8 Chevy, a wife, children, and a steady, though unrewarding job. Like most of his friends, he was of the white ethnic working class with a father who worked for the Union Pacific or Swift & Company. High school and his carefully bordered delinquency provided a pastoral interlude before the weight of lower-middle American life settled in on him. They offered gaiety and a reckless freedom, if only briefly, to an almost completely predictable life. He was, in the words of the song he sang on his way to the assistant principal's office from the study hall, rocking around the clock, with all the dedication and sense of limitation that implies.

"come on baby, let the good times roll"

Come on baby
Let the good times roll,
Come on baby
Let me thrill your soul,
Come on baby
Let the good times roll
Roll all night long.

Late October on a bluff over the river, the tincture of wet leaves in the night air, river fog below, thick smoke from wet kindling in a bonfire, hot dogs and marshmallows on straightened coat hangers, touch football in a small meadow, some nestling down in the park department pavilion, enthralled touch-ups in the wet darkness beyond the ring of tall trees. Just past the pavilion the bluff knuckles down to the river road, a flat of farmed-out silt beside it like a stubbled margin, then the Missouri, lustrous as damp skin, bridge lights pillowed in haze. Sparks reel upward; hot dogs fizzle; marshmallows shed successions of charred husks. It could have been a movie, a few frames before the monster oozes up out of the fog or the flying saucer scorches its nest into the brush: perfect American teenaged fun—food, football, music from a 45rpm Webcor portable, wired out the pavilion doorway, two girls in pedal pushers dancing (obviously the monster will get them first for being so careless with their loneliness).

The football game begins to collapse. Passes spiral into the trees, and the game stops regularly while the ball is recovered. A group of girls invade the meadow, and two-handed touch becomes a loose game of tag. Everyone is "it." I chase a girl named Caroline, a blonde in flowered slacks and a pink angora sweater. My fingers brush her shoulder.

"Caught you."

"Did not."

She is panting, hands on her knees, face turned up, blond hair wisped around her eyes, her breath clouding the air between us like a gauze filter in a love scene. She leans one way, then runs the other, a pink and floral offensive guard, a play-maker. This time I slap the back of her sweater solidly.

"There!"

"You have to catch me," she shouts back, heading toward the trees, hair spinning. I tackle her at the waist and roll to the side, landing on my back on the wet grass.

"Can't catch me, can't catch me."

She is lying across me, the small of her back against my stomach. One of my arms is across her waist; the other is caught between her thighs. Bits of leaf and grass are suspended in her hair. She stares up at the sky.

"Can't catch me."

A slight movement, not at all calculated, and my arm moves between her legs, nestling upward. There is an immediate, fearful recoil, and suddenly my bare wrist is pressed into her crotch, hand extended awkwardly into the night behind her, perspiring, cold. I wait for her to react. She does not. I want to move, not move, pull my hand out, through, fingers settling where my wrist warms intolerably, hold still forever. Everything is still. The whole evening seems suspended around the peculiar sensation on my wrist.

"Can't catch me," she says again, faintly this time, like a secret held between us. "Can't catch me." She is smiling and has crossed her legs to hold me fast. I move a little, as though preparing to lift her, and she arches against me to hold me down. There is a bone there for my pulse to beat against—soft, hard, warm, a moist disk, made more acute by the terrible chill, the paralysis of my hand and fingers. There is nothing I can do that will not end it all, that will not impel us into the painful cycle of accusation and apology that goes with drive-in-movie second features. I imagine that by now it glows with her, that place on the wrist mothers offer to test warmed baby's milk.

"We should go back now." It is another voice, full of feigned certainty and school. Her legs are uncrossed, and she is instantly off me, standing, picking the broken fragments of autumn from her sweater as though it were lint. I pull the webbed cuff of my jacket down over my wrist and stand up. Back at the bonfire, she slips easily into the party, out of reach.

"What you been doin' out there, man?"

"Nothin'."

"Then, how come you're so messed up?"

"Don't worry about it, hear."

"Don't matter none to me."

"Football."

"What?"

"Touch football, that's how I got so messed up."

"Oh."

I wanted a corner where I could look at it, touch it, a place where I could peel my jacket cuff slowly back so as not to disturb what still burned there. I ate a hot dog with my left hand and looked for her through the smoke. She was talking to three other girls. I think that at least once she saw me staring and turned away. She was embarrassed or ashamed, I thought. Or disgusted with me for my hesitation. *Can't catch me.* And after all, I hadn't caught her, only a handful of nightchill, that and the token she pressed into my pulse. Dead fish, they always said. I remembered by uncle's story about the woman in his rooming house, naked across her bed, knees up, door wide open—"airing out her cunt," he said. I pushed my hand through my hair and inhaled. Nothing but the wincing sharpness of the campfire smoke and the rich mulchy decay of wet leaves and withering grass. Later, much later, at home in the dark, the memory of bread dough rising under damp towels in a closed kitchen.

Longing is the priest of names. "O Caroline, Caroline"—that night I said her name over and over to myself in the dark, wrist warming to each syllable, reeling like Washington above his pots and pans at the back of the Castle Hotel kitchen, a sweetness as sure as Muscatel snagging at the back of my tongue. "Caroline"—thighs bared to the sound of it, bare breasts and wet leaves, bits of wet grass, and, dear God, the soft brown curling damp hair between her legs tendriled down into my wrist like seed sprouts penetrating fresh soil, the air around us thick with yeast and warm except for that black space behind her where my cold fingers still grappled at the dark. "Bitch," I said out loud, something caught hold of in the chill night air and clutched firmly like a buoy and a life ring. It pulled me away from her, and I sat up in bed and wished the whole thing had never happened and wished, as well, to burrow back down into the dream. "Bitch. Whore. Cunt. Caroline." "Mus . . . ah . . . ever . . . tell"—Washington with his wet hand warping the starched sleeve of my bus coat, pleading with me for a can of cold blue iridescent Sterno to keep his monsters at bay. "You keep after that shit, man, you gonna go blind"—Whiskey-Nose Louie calling to Washington? Love is blind. "Whore." "Get yourself a good whore, boy, and you'll never go wrong." "Mus . . . ah . . . ever . . . never . . . tell." All wrong—my failure in the meadow (should have just grabbed it) walking back, sulking off into a corner, this lovesick crap, whining her name, and wrong, too, to want so badly for it all to go away. "Cunt."

At school the next week she acted as though nothing had

happened between us. She was genial and indifferent. I hated her for her aloofness, for not offering me some small gesture, a smile, an inflection, anything, and I hated myself for attaching so much importance to it all and for needing her so desperately to credit it somehow. If cool was the game, then she had won. Or perhaps it wasn't cool at all but genuine indifference. I would watch for her in the hall, notebook held to her front like a breastplate, her white, lace-edged collar dolloped over the neck of another frothy sweater, thinking of what I might have done in that meadow, and she would pass by, nodding to her friends without so much as a glance. She lived on the hill above the school in a white frame house with flower beds and a front porch, far from the projects and Twenty-fourth Street, and that distance scraped at my feelings about her.

In the late winter she called me to ask a favor. She wanted a copy of a "Negro" record and asked me if I could buy it for her. There was an absolute division then between white and "brown" music; rhythm and blues was kept off the radio and out of the downtown stores. The next day I went to the A & A Music Company on Lake Street and bought her a copy of "Let the Good Times Roll." The day after that I carried it to her house, believing that the request was at long last a token of our autumn encounter and that she meant the words of the song to speak to me—"feels so good, when you're near." And nearer to her, I was suddenly sure that her call was part of an elaborate joke at my expense. Lumps of snow clung to the springs of the bare porch-glider frame. The monogrammed aluminum storm strained inward as the mahogany door behind it was pulled open. Caroline. Her friend Renee was right behind her, grinning.

"Would you like to sit down?"

I pushed the record her way and said something about work.

"Well, thanks for the record," she said down into the sack. Renee was nodding. The rhinestone eye of the black panther on the television set flickered in my direction. I looked down at the bits of snow and slush sliding down across the toes of my boots and falling onto the sculptured rose carpet. Stupid, once again. There had been no secret message in the song, nothing in her request at all but the record itself. It would almost have been better if it had been a joke and five or six more of them had popped up from behind the furniture to laugh at my gullibility, but there was only Renee with all the awkward eagerness of a cocker spaniel.

"It was nothing, really." I made my way to the bus stop through the dingy snow, certain that she had got Renee over there to keep me from staying and from getting the wrong idea.

At the music shop my friend Emmett, one of the A's in A & A had asked me what I was doing buying Dick and Dee Dee.

"It's for a friend."

"Fluff?"

"Yeah."

"Cottonwood fluff?"

"Uh-huh."

"Man, all you's buyin' is trouble."

"What you mean?"

"Look here. What's this here bit of cottonwood want with a little lowdown and dirty? Take my advice. Get her a Teresa Brewer."

"She asked for Dick and Dee Dee."

"Shoot, man, you're in worse trouble than I thought. Asked for it . . . motherjump. Man, I don't know if you're ready for this. You gonna roll all night long, huh? That what you figure she's askin' for?" .

"I . . . uh . . . I don't know."

"Fuckin' A, you don't know. You watch out or you gonna get turned every way but up. Man, I don't know either, some bit a cottonwood fluff wants to get low down, sends you round here to old uncle Emmett with your hands in your pockets . . . every way but up, Jack, you'll see."

Half a minute at the door, and it was over, four months of whispering her name, scouting her out in the hallway at school, hurrying so I could brush past her, rehearsed conversations, telephone calls half-dialed, the swirling trail back to the meadow, a hundred alternate endings, "Come on baby." . . . —the skin on my wrist pink and tender as the warm sticky surface beneath a fresh blister, wounded like the sacred heart in my father's medallion, golden rays of sunlight all around, thorns wound tight, drops of blood like melting rubies, cold, bloodless fingers, St. Peter reaching upward from the waves— ". . . all night long."

The curbside snow had been hardened into grit by the sun. The sidewalk was wet with melting snow. With the toe of my boot I broke scallops of blackened ice off the sharp edge of the gray mound beside the signboard bench. OMAR'S BREAD, FRESH TO YOUR DOOR. I pushed my foot, heel first, through the hard, grainy crust. It crunched like broken glass on asphalt, then softened. Inside it was still soft and white. Between the cut-out my foot had made in the dark surface and the gray bruise it left inside, there was a bright halo of pure white. I thought for a minute that I would press my wrist into it, turning my wound against its perfect cold, but I was embarrassed for even thinking such a thing and looked around to see if anyone had seen me think it. Cars hissed by on the wet street, graceful and oblivious.

Back in her bedroom, baby blue with cornflower prints and white chiffon, the record fell onto the black rubber treads of an RCA 45 rpm portable's turntable, and the blue plastic tone arm jerked into place. Renee preened her spit curls in the mirror above the blue and white kick-skirted vanity, and Caroline leaned back on the bed, her head propped on one hand, elbow creasing a cornflower-and-lace-covered pillow. I tried to imagine her thoughts as she listened to Dee Dee sing, "Fee-ohs so goo-oo-ood," as though the phrase were a nerve she stretched tight and played—nothing but faint shadows of the autumn meadow along the edges of the spring-blue bedroom and bits of broken leaves imposed on the ponytail that swayed gently along her forearm.

The next week Emmett followed me into Merritt's drugstore to ask what had happened with the record. I began a self-serving lie that quickly trailed off into a mutter.

"Took the record and shut the door in your face, right?"

"Almost."

What did I tell you, man? What . . . did . . . I . . . tell . . . you! Roll all night long, huh?"

"Somethin' like that."

"Every way but up."

"How could you be so sure she'd shut me out?"

"Man, that's just the way it is with cottonwood fluff. You try to catch it in the air man, and it floats right through your fingers. Wait till it settles and you can have all you want."

"What's that supposed to mean?"

"It means be cool cause it ain't your problem."

"Well, she led me on."

"Listen to you, boy. What you think this is, a picture show? You got tickled a little, that's all, and it didn't cost you but eighty-nine cents. Count yourself lucky."

"Well, if she didn't mean nothin', why'd she pick that song."

"Now, that's another thing altogether." He motioned toward the fountain, sat down, and ordered a plain seltzer. Lots a these chicks like lowdown music, man, and they like it real black, you know what I mean? Now, that don't mean they're hot for some black cat or for any white cat either. They just want to play dirty man, and they ain't nothin' washes off easier than somebody else's dirt. See what I mean? It's like it ain't got nothin' to do with her, so she can do all she wants. Bet she likes that redneck Presley."

"Guess so."

"Same difference. This chick ever be caught dead with a greasehead peckerwood like Elvis?

"Naw."

"See what I mean, same difference."

"Well, it ain't fair."

"Fair don't mean shit in a barnyard. If it was fair, they'd all be diggin' on me, 'stead a on them fuckin' records or diggin' on you 'stead a that wiggleass peckerwood who cain't half-play that guitar he humps around on."

He brought his nickel-plated paper cup holder down on the marble counter like a gavel—court adjourned—stood up, and shook out the pleats of his charcoal gabardines. "Hang loose, hear?"

"All we can do is try." It was one of his expressions offered as a muted thank-you.

"That's straight."

Still, the Breck Girl on the faded, waterstained card propped in the drugstore window leaned her loose blond hair in my direction, as soft and cool as June Christy whispering or Julie London breathing a half-beat rest. O Caroline.

a real bomb

Just south of Omaha, spread out across an old Army Air Corps base and a Martin bomber plant, overshadowing the small river towns of Plattsmouth and Bellevue, Offutt Air Force Base, headquarters of the Strategic Air Command, with multifloored office buildings sunk deep into the river's clay bluffs. If there was a single button that could ignite the American nuclear arsenal, it was in one of those buildings. Offutt would be, we were always told with some pride, the prime target of the first wave of a Russian attack. That strip of sheared-off bluff, where Lewis and Clark once hunted for deer, would sprout mushroom clouds like an old log on a rainy day opening out concentric circles of fire strong enough to enfold us all. Because so much of the base was buried in the ground, Offutt never looked imposing enough to have the world's fate in its control, just a scattering of low buildings behind a Cyclone fence with a few hangars in the background. At the gate there was a billboard with SAC's emblem, an armored fist full of thunderbolts, a mixture of archaic technology and myth, as though a Thor or Zeus were housed inside. Or was it merely masculine bravado, spiked iron knuckles in place of a poised index finger.

During the 1950s Curtis LeMay was commander of SAC. In those years he was a sports car fanatic. He built a figure-eight track across the runways and held a *grand prix* race with cars and drivers flown in from all over the world. He raced his own formula cars up and down the airstrip and was frequently photographed in one of the hangars tinkering at his Offenhauser, his square face and permanently stubbed cigar, suggesting despite the jowls a World War II flight commander straight out of *Command Decision* or Steve Canyon transposed into an alien environment of sharp B-47 wing sweeps and tail angles. There was something in the way LeMay jutted himself into the world that was both frightening and reassuring. He acted as though he believed that the entire tangle of what Air Force training manuals called *global politics* was susceptible to his swagger, as though guts could manage it all, guts and style. It was frightening to anyone steeped in the idea that we were all just minutes away from atomic destruction, since LeMay's posturing made the man at the button look just seconds away from his next barroom brawl. It was reassuring because if you chose, even briefly, to accept this John Wayne view of things, the Cold War seemed a bit more comprehensible. It is no surprise that LeMay's only public surfacing after his retirement was as George Wallace's running mate on the American Independent Party's ticket in 1968. LeMay's posturing and Wallace's were essentially the same. Whatever their private cynicisms, both men seemed willing to take on America's problems and all of its enemies toe-to-toe.

LeMay's love of cars and the fashion he led for speedsters among SAC pilots involve a curious paradox. Sitting at SAC's ultimate button or at the controls of a B-36 would seem enough power to have as it is proliferated from one set of hands outward through the lattices of modern technology. Still, there was in LeMay—and in his pilots—just as there was in so many

American teenagers, the unshaken sense that technology's most personal, most responsive implement of individual power was a sleek, highly-polished, well-tuned car. You could imagine LeMay at work all day in front of a polar map of the world with Russian targets and American bomber squadrons lit from behind, waiting for the NORAD communications system to flash the first Russian planes across the DEW line—Distant Early Warning, that arc at the top of the world that had become America's new northern border, a line drawn not for customs or immigration but the threshold of nuclear hysteria, the chip we had placed on the ice shoulder of the glove—and while he sat there in the War Room, at the seventh subterranean level of the Offutt Administration Building, his mind would wander, just as ours did in school, from industrial complexes and second-strike capabilities to carburetors and intake manifolds. Beyond the bustle of his aides and the chatter of the teletype machines, he could hear an engine revving up tight, the throbbing center of the machine American English calls *she* redlining to the edge of her endurance, then gulping in one great breath quickly as the gears are shifted and beginning that long, high song once again. It was his *melos* and ours—Ferrari and Offenhauser or Olds and Merc, sirens' songs, the formula soprano of the *grand prix* or the guttural funk of glass packs or Smitty's backing off down the Burt Street hill behind Technical High School, enough to turn every head in class and spring enthusiasts out of their seats and to the windows, Chevy sixes with split manifolds that could splat school windows until they rattled in their frames, the low thunder of an early Olds 88 with its tightened Hydra-Matic transmission pulled down into "Lo" gear, Mercurys with chrome resonators bubbling like Chrysler marine inboard engines, the Detroit falsetto of tires screeching out of the parking lot at midday as the shop-class students peeled off to afternoons as apprentice factory workers, the exhaust tattoo of cars each afternoon, muscling their leaded decks and whitewalls past crowded sidewalks at the end of the day.

* * *

Chevrolet '49 deluxe 4-door $245
* * *

Chevrolet '49 2-door, radio, heater $195
* * *

Ford '49 club $95
* * *

Ford '41 deluxe Tudor, radio, heater. Good body $135
* * *

Oldsmobile '49 88, radio, heater,
Hydra-Matic. Only $345
* * *

Plymouth '49 2-door $195
* * *

'48 Mercury, club	$79
'47 Plymouth, real good	$79
'46 Ford, A-1	$79
'41 Dodge	$39
'47 Ford, as is	$39
'36 Plymouth, good	$35
'35 Ford, O.K.	$39

WE TRADE FOR WATCHES,
DIAMONDS, FURNITURE
MOTORCYCLES OR ANYTHING
TRY US!

* * *

After the rush hour, when the hotel kitchen settled down, I would sit at the stainless steel salad table, boxed in by refrigerator doors and shelves of clean glasses, and study the classified ads in the newspaper for affordable and acceptable cars. Acceptable was determined by social and esthetic values, not just by mechanical considerations. There were hulking, old, family sedans around that were quite cheap and sound, lumbering 1940's Dodges, DeSotos, sloshy Buick Roadmasters with Dynaflow transmissions, Hudsons, Packards, Studebakers, and Ford and Mercury 4-doors that looked like the hunchbacked police cars in Boston Blackie movies. Two-doors were better; club coupes were best. That '49 Chevy 2-door with radio and heater would be fine, especially if it were a slantback, and the Ford coupes would do. The prize in the paper was the '49 Olds 88 Hydra-Matic, but it was priced like a prize. At $345 it was out of the question. I wanted to spend less than $150, and so scouted the "WE TRADE FOR WATCHES . . . ANYTHING" ad. I thought about the '35 Ford, in its own way another kind of prize, a hotrodder's dream, but it would take more than $111 to make a '35 respectable. I settled on the '41 Ford deluxe Tudor with a good body. It would just take a little bit of money, a little work, and I'd be on the street. Maybe I could talk him down the cost of a glass pack muffler and a set of seat covers. I thought about the flared, sharp-nosed grill of the '41 Ford and the dowelled crossbars of the '46 Ford, A-1.

"Gonna get a car?" Ray, the salad man, sliding a bucket of Thousand Island dressing onto the other end of the table.

"Yeah."

"You old enough to drive yet?"

"Next summer."

"You ought to get one a them pussy wagons like Sammy's got." Sammy was a pot washer always getting ready to go to Las Vegas. He drove a black '53 Pontiac convertible. "Ain't much a woman won't do to ride in a convertible. It's just like bein' on the stage."

"If I was buyin' a car, I'd get me one a them Nash Ramblers, 'cause the seats go all the way down to make a double bed. You be sittin' there with your girl, and you just push this button, and zip, man, you got her in bed." Jimmy, a busboy from the South Side joins in.

"Ford," says Paul, like a bullfrog croaking. "Get a Ford. Best car. Ford. I got a Ford. Drive it all the time."

"Paul, you ain't got a car."

"Yes, I do. Got a Ford. Best car."

"Then where is it? How come nobody here ever seen you drivin' it?"

"Fifty-two Ford, blue and white. Best car."

"If you got a car, where the fuck is it?"

"Garage. I keep in in the garage. Ford. Get a Ford. Best car. Fifty-two Ford."

"He ain't got no Ford. He ain't got any kind a car."

"What you want with a car?" Hilda, waiting for a chef's salad bowl in her puckered pink nylon uniform with a white lace handkerchief ironed into a sharp triangle pinned over one ample breast.

"Just to get around in."

"Just to get a little in. These high school girls nowadays don't do shit for a guy that ain't got a car. Ain't that right, kid?"

Hilda put the salad bowl on a dinner plate and arranged three cellophane packages of crackers around the edge. "Honey, there's a whole lot a things girls like more than cars."

My uncle called late one night to say that a guy he worked with had a '48 Plymouth Tudor he would sell for $125 and that we could probably talk him down to $100. He said he would drive me out to look at it the next night I had off and told me to get $110 in cash, just in case. He brought his brother-in-law, Junior, along to drive the Plymouth back if we bought it. The car was in Plattesmouth in the barnyard of a small truck farm. The farmer turned on a floodlight above the barn door, but the car was still shadowed behind a hay wagon. My uncle got in and started it. The exhaust burbled like a four-stroke Mercury outboard. "My kid put one a them damned Smitty's on there just before he went to the service. 'S got a '48 Dodge engine, mud tires in the back, and fog lights." He reached past my uncle and switched on the amber fog lights fixed to the front bumper. The weeded edge of his field glowed bright gold. "Radio works." My uncle switched on the radio. It hummed for a few seconds, then the music came on. I still hadn't been inside the car. I walked around and looked at the tires, pushed down on the front fender for the feel of the shocks. I opened the passenger door, pushed the seat back forward, and looked into the backseat. My uncle shut the engine off.

"Wanna try it?"

I got in, turned the key, and pressed the starter. One turn and it was going. I could feel the turning of the engine surge a little at the car when I revved it, then let up and waited for that single, steel-wool-filled Smitty to belch a bit as the engine slowed. I rolled the window down to see how it felt with my elbow out, right wrist hooked over the top of the steering wheel.

"Let's go inside."

The four of us sat down at the farmer's enameled kitchen table. His wife was standing on the worn black stretch of linoleum in front of the sink, snapping beans. An old barnyard collie with matted hair paced a while, then curled up in the doorway to the front room. My uncle said, "A hundred."

"You know it's my son's car. Wrote me from San Diego to sell the car. Said I should get a hundred and a quarter."

"A hundred and ten."

"Got himself another car out there."

"A hundred and ten."

"Runs real good."

"A hundred and ten."

"Okay."

I hadn't said a word since we got out of my uncle's car. After months of looking through the papers and stopping by used car lots, it all seemed too abrupt. I counted the money out onto the table and shook hands with the farmer, then rode back to town on the passenger side of my new car. We listened to the radio. Junior drove to my house, and my mother came out and looked at it parked by the plaza stairs on Twenty-second Street. She said it looked nice. Then Junior drove it off to my uncle's backyard, where it would wait for driving lessons and my sixteenth birthday.

I didn't see it again until the next week. I rode over on the bus. In the daylight it was a different car. It was pea green, but the paint was chalked from the weather. The floor mats were caked with mud, and the driver's seat was worn through to the springs. Sometimes the clutch stuck to the floor and had to be nudged loose with the sole of my shoe, then quickly caught before it had sprung out completely, lurching the car into a stall. All the outside chrome had a filmy look to it, and the windshield had begun to discolor a bit at the edges. I started it and ran the engine fast, leaning back out the open door to listen to the exhaust pipe bubble. It took the edge off my disappointment.

Buffed with rubbing compound and carefully waxed with a cushion stuffed into the hole in the front seat and covered with $5.95 worth of wickered hemp seat covering, it made a respectable car, but it was not by any stretch of the imagination a *machine*. I bought a 100-pound bag of sand from a lumberyard for the trunk, just to get its rear end down a little, and bought a chrome exhaust extension that was shaped like a kerosene lamp chimney and gave the exhaust's bubbling a bit more resonance. I was sorry I had not held out for a Ford V-8 or a Plymouth Club Coupe. But it ran well. The voltage regulator stuck sometimes. When I noticed it on the ampmeter, I could fix it by opening the hood and tapping the regulator with my comb. And it would vapor-lock on hot days, but I carried a jar of water in the trunk, and if it stalled in the heat, I poured the water over the fuel pump, and it would start again. Sometimes I talked abut dropping a bigger engine in her but never intended to and once considered stripping the chrome ornaments off the hood and trunk; nosing and decking was what it was called. The idea was to take all the chrome off a car and fill the holes, then smooth it out and repaint it. Then I could shackle the rear end, meaning tie down the rear leaf springs with U-shaped shackles that would give the car the appearance of being perpetually overloaded or—and this was the real purpose, I guess—make it look, even at curbside, as though it were in the midst of its first drag strip acceleration. A really serious person with a more workable car—a Ford coupe or a Mercury Tudor—

would have chopped the roof posts in half, lowering the windshield into the sort of eye slits seen on armored vehicles in movies about the Africa Corps, and channeled the body down into the chassis.

Removing the chrome and smoothing out the car's lines created out of clumsy forties club coupes missiles of strange proportions, not so much rocket profiles, though that seemed to be one goal that was strived for as bullets, .38 dum-dums, canted slightly upward. An earlier generation of young drivers over–ornamented their cars, fitting them with external chrome horns, mirrors, radio antennas with raccoon tails, working, as much as possible, against the car's line of motion, front to back. In the fifties the impulse was to smooth the car into a single uncluttered mass. The jalopy had been replaced by the bomb. In extremely refined circumstances the chrome was replaced with pin striping. The flow lines of air across its laquered skin were remade in thin, painted lines that swirled or feathered around headlights and taillights like the vortices smoke makes as it eddies around an airfoil in a wind tunnel. At their most extreme these were embellished into red, orange, and yellow flames that seemed to burst the cars they decorated straight out of hell and down the street.

If you liked chrome, you could fill the engine compartment with it. There were chrome breathers for most carburetors, chrome manifolds, and chrome nut covers for the nuts that held the top of the engine down. For Fords and Chevys with tin tappet covers over the top of the engine, there were full chrome lids. You were supposed to keep the engine clean. There was a gunk you could slop over the engine block with a paintbrush, and the old grease and dirt would melt away, or you could pay $4.95 and have your engine steam-cleaned at a garage downtown. A clean, shining engine was a sign of devotion, cosmetic and ritualistic. For performance, there were catalogs full of speed equipment—compression kits, racing cams, headers, hardened rings, cylinder sleeves, pitched manifolds, little chrome cannister down-draft carburetors, transmission kits, locking differentials, spark boosters, and extra hot coils. Only a few people worked at the engines of their cars. Appearance came first, then sound. Dual exhausts running from each of the manifolds of a V-8 made the sweetest sound. Split manifold sixes were fine. There were also kits with flex pipes that would deflect half the exhaust just above the muffler. Mufflers came in hundreds of shapes and sounds. Smitty's were the most aggressive, then came a variety of glass packs, steel tomato juice cans filled with fiberglass home insulation.

The desire to modify cars makes obvious sense. If the car was the maximum shape technology offered to the individual, then it needed to be made new, if only in accepted, fashionable ways. My guess is that we remade our cars or, lacking the resources, dreamed of remaking them in our own image, projecting through them an enlarged version of what we wanted to be. The sleek, customized cars of the fifties sculpted the cool everyone aspired to, that edgeless demeanor that specialized in minimal lateral gestures and latent violence. The smooth backward flow of bright metal matched the sweep of oiled ducktails and the flare of turned-up shirt collars.

In *Rebel Without a Cause*, James Dean spent his first day at his new school dressed in a jacket and tie. His appearance and his opening drunk scene made him curious, even interesting, but his potential energy in the film was not fully indicated until he was seen with his car, a customized '49 Mercury, nosed and decked with guttural, dual exhausts. The ambivalence of Dean's character exists in the subcultural space between his soft, tentative manner and the accomplished aggression of one of that era's perfect cars, perfectly executed. His distinctness had for its emblem the red nylon jacket he wore for the rest of the film. Dean's antagonist, Buzz, wore a black leather jacket, the sign of a deeper social rebelliousness and a different set of class aspirations.

In the process of elevating Dean's vulnerability, the movie degraded the black leather jacket. Buzz's jacket is the cause of his death in the chicken run with Dean. At the moment he decided to jump from his car, the cuff strap of his jacket was caught in the door handle. His car went over the cliff while he struggled to free it. Dean jumped to safety in the meadow. Black leather was the armor of the teenaged extremist, *The Wild One*. *Rebel Without a Cause* was a centrist movie that offered a retreat from extremes. Dean could redeem himself by leaving his car, not just the chicken-run jalopy speeding toward the cliff, but his perfect Mercury as well. His first romantic moment with Natalie Wood occurred outside as he swung childishly from the branch of a small tree. In the abandoned mansion, Dean and Wood played house, with Sal Mineo as their disturbed child. Like a number of other important movies of the same period—*Shane* and *High Noon*, most notably—*Rebel Without a Cause* dealt with the conflict between masculine honor and domestic values. Dean's Mercury certified him to the movie's audience. It invested him with an unquestioned cool. That red jacket, which was immediately taken up as a part of the standard wardrobe and sold out nationally in a matter of days, was important to the movie's conservative resolution of the conflicting values it portrayed. Dean's stylized tenderness, the winning innocence of his faltering sexual gestures toward Natalie Wood, and his idealized role as father to Sal Mineo offered a model for the domestic values to which most kids still subscribed. For Dean and Wood, the family was an essential, positive structure that was being mismanaged by insensitive and cowardly adults. Both of *Rebel's* extremists are killed off at the edges of things: Buzz, with his jacket hooked to a door handle, drove off the end of America, and Mineo, who was the failed family's complete victim, died on the steps of an observatory, afraid of the universe. Dean was no rebel but a conservative hero, more conservative than Gary Cooper in *High Noon*, who accepted the isolation of honor, or Alan Ladd in *Shane*, who knew that once resurrected his gun would bar him from the domesticity it was used to save. Dean's only rebellious figure was his car. Perfectly stylized, it was a gesture, like cool, more studied retreat than rebellion.

Although the society generally saw hot rods and custom cars as antisocial and heard modified exhaust systems as wordless blasphemies, in retrospect the rod and custom craze hardly seems rebellious. Ideally, the hot rodder improved the car he bought, whether it was new or old. Engines were altered or replaced, cleaned and lavished with chrome. Every engineering change in Detroit had compensating modifications that quickly entered the teenaged, oral tradition. Everyone knew how the bands of a GM could be tightened for greater acceleration and knew the boring and stroking tolerances of new Ford V-8's to the thousandth of an inch. Smoothing out a car's surfaces was a lead Detroit eventually followed, and it is not hard to see the customizing impulses of the fifties in the "personal" cars from Detroit in the sixties. The range of engine and transmission options that were developed had Detroit selling its own bombs from the showroom, customized small auto bodies with enormous engines, superlethal Plymouths, Dodges, Fords, and Chevys. Oldsmobile produced a street car that would burn a mixture of alcohol and ether when the accelerator was pressed to the floor. It was an option on their 1964 F-86. F-86 was the official designation of the American Sabre Jet in the Korean War. Other similar, stock hot rods also had names that would appeal to the driver's unrequited aggressions—Mustang, Javelin, Cougar, Barracuda, Firebird, Fury. American Motors had a car scheduled for production that was to have been called the Banshee, until someone in the company discovered that a banshee was an angel of death whose approach was signaled by a long, high-pitched screech. The name, it was said, was abandoned because it was nearer reality than fantasy. More modest automobiles, designed for family life, were given names to suit the reveries of their intended owners. The residents of housing tracts were sold Bel Airs and Biscaynes or station wagons called Country Squires and Estate Wagons. For the unsettled and more fanciful, there were Monte Carlos and Monacos; for the devil-may-care, Grand Prixs, Bonnevilles, and GTOs, and out in the distance, as ever, beyond reach, Eldorado, a City of Gold with Cruise Control and front wheel drive. The teenaged car culture of the fifties was noisy and dangerous, but it was not rebellious. It was an eager, sometimes raucous preparation for the future.

The ostensibly delinquent hotrodder of the fifties, defined by his modified car, seems now something of a pioneer in the development of the American sensibility about the car. He helped transform the car from its prewar stability and familial permanence to the devoutly held, but transient thing it had, necessarily, to become. He also helped make it more conspicuously a machine. With almost Bauhaus purity, he removed everything that was extraneous to the car's function—its function having been redefined not as transportation but as speed. All those elaborate exhaust systems were designed to amplify and revel in the sounds of the internal combustion engine. The endless cleaning and chroming of engine parts enshrined the mechanism itself, and the profile customizing most often sought, offered a sense of motion, even when the car was standing still. Of course, all of this was a highly mannered version of speed. The years since have developed much more gawky but highly efficient styles—dragsters with rear ends boosted up over heavy springs, their noses canted downward, wide, treadless tires, and pitched aerodynamic spoilers. Clearly, the fifties car was inefficient in its sense of speed and high performance, but it was an esthetic period in which the machine and its power were given romantic shape and contour.

The first night I drove my Plymouth home from the hotel I went down Fifteenth Street just to listen to the song of the mud tires on the brick pavement and the flaring, derbied trumpet doo-wa 's of the exhaust passing darkened buildings. It was a perfect drive, the brickwork street, empty and shining in the streetlights like softly rippled calm water. Traffic lights flicked green all the way to Cummings Street. I drove west, past school to the drive-in, toured the lot once, then backed into an empty stall to order a cheeseburger and a marshmallow milkshake. I slid down under the wheel a bit and waited to be recognized. My friend Fred, who worked in the drive-in kitchen, came out to see it. He wiped his hands on his apron and leaned into the passenger window. "It's a heap," he said, "a real heap." At home, parked at the base of the plaza stairs, I tested three or four driving postures in the dark, let my wrist hang loosely over the top of the steering wheel, pulled my hand back and caught the wheel with my fingertips, then dropped my arm until my hand was bent back, sat forward and clasped the base of the wheel with both hands. I even tried turning to the side, like the South Side hotrodders, with my right forearm resting on the wheel and my left hand extended below the dashboard along the firewall. The amber-clouded radio dial glowed like a new horizon. Heap or not, I had entered the world of cars, of drive-in movies, and hilltop lovers' lanes. I touched the near center of the seat beside me and imagined her there, any her, conspicuously close. The engine crackled a little as it cooled, nestling in for the night.

"life could be a dream, sweetheart"

Out of confusion perhaps or terror or confused pleasure bordering on terror, Laura told Patti. And Patti told Ron. And Ron told everyone.

In the fourth-floor hall, where cool was traded each day like stocks on Wall Street, Alvin and his friends leaned against gray lockers in plaid McGregor shirts buttoned at the neck and Big D denims and sucked long kisses out at Phil whenever he passed. "Eat-a-box," they called him, "Eat-a-box Phil," slurping like straws circling the bottoms of empty paper cups. Girls in groups of three or four swung by, three-ring notebooks held tightly into their waists, straight skirts cupped, slightly, under their buttocks, kick-pleats twitching across freshly shaven calves. Younger boys weaved around them, spiral notebooks and textbooks held at their sides, shoulders dipping their moves from side to side lake skaters in a crowded roller rink. Cool blacks in bib overalls, pink Mr. B. shirts, charcoal-black knit ties, and one-button roll powder blue sport coats bobbed in their own corner by the stairs. Cigarette smoke billowed from the bathroom door each time it swung open and boiled in the light from the stairwell behind them.

"Eat-a-box." Everything stopped for half a second and turned toward Phil as he quickly made the corner into class. Laura moved anonymously in a circle of girls, her blond bangs in tight Mamie Eisenhower curls. The hallway resumed its random business. They had been yearbook steadies, the sort of couple that turned up several times in the snapshot collages at the back of the book entitled *Summer Daze*, mugging up from a beach towel or waving from a canoe. She was quiet and precise, a persistent class secretary from the middle class hillside, west of the school. He was from the river bottoms, buoyed up out of the impossibilities of his neighborhood by a studied manner. He worked in a clothing store on weekends and in a restaurant at night, drove an unassuming Nash, and wore pressed Levi's and tailored sport shirts. Their relationship had had about it the calm reliability girls called cute. They were a cute couple without the threat of passion so many others posed, affectionately asexual, it seemed, two "really swell personalities" discretely holding hands.

That fall, a few days before Eisenhower's second election, they skipped the meetings of the second day of the State High School Speech Conference, playing hooky alone in a room in the finest hotel in Lincoln, Nebraska. They closed the venetian blinds, no doubt, pulled the drapes, and bolted the top lock on the door. Whether his descent across her stomach moved smoothly or faltered, no one knew. Or whether, if it faltered, it was his indecision or her modesty that caused the delay or a subtle dalliance, a reassuring look upward to soothe her apprehension, pale, trembling fingers extended to rearrange his tousled hair, a fingertip trailed softly across his temple, resting a moment on his cheek. Or if she lifted herself toward him or arched away, if he held her and for how long. She told Patti simply that it had happened and that she didn't know what to do.

When the taunts in the corridor began, Phil and Laura

stopped seeing each other. Phil went to class each day, crisply. He never answered or even acknowledged the fourth floor's slurping condemnations. The few friends he kept were cherished, and there was an undercurrent of gratitude to being with him that made you feel both virtuous and slightly uncomfortable. He never mentioned the episode in the hotel and refused to speak to anyone who brought up the subject. His manners had always been careful and slightly adult, with a hint of the calculated chuminess that goes with clothing stores. They were his way of keeping the stain of East Omaha and a childhood shared with Harlowe Brown at arm's length. As the victim of the school's collective fear and hatred, he grew stylish, as though he had found a way of surviving in a Stewart Granger movie on the late show. He dressed in slacks and V-neck sweaters over button-down shirts open at the neck. The antagonisms in the hallway were inflamed by his refusal to acknowledge them. "Cunt-eater," they said, younger accusers dancing out into his path, aiming their long, sucking sounds directly into his face. He walked around them.

Laura moved through school hived in a circle of girls, friends who offered her the disdain-filled altruism they usually spent on the pathetically ugly or the affably fat. She had become as much of an outsider as he had, but no accusation or derision was turned on her. She was somehow excused as victim and was spared even the secret longing and late, anonymous telephone calls that went to girls who were said to have *done it*, the standard *it*, the ones who *came across* and *put out*. Who could dream of Laura without dreaming of his face locked there where Phil's had been. She seemed immensely sad and disconnected, as though she had been removed from the center of her own life as well as from the center of the social life around her. No boyfriend arrived to take Phil's place. In the winter I was asked to a party at her house. It was clearly her parents' doing, a last resort, and they hovered at the edges of the awkward gathering like parents watching a frail, sickly child at play. Her father shook my hand several times and said that he had heard a great deal about me. It was the first time I had ever been invited there. It wasn't the sort of place I was asked to come to, fresh and cheery, like Ozzie and Harriet's house, all cookies and sweet fruit punch, with ping-pong and bumper pool in the finished basement. I thought, at first, that I had been invited because I was Phil's friend but decided after I arrived that I was there because I was another kind of outsider. It all had the forced gaiety of Sunday-school socials, and I left early.

Phil seemed to weather it all. He worked and studied. One night after we both finished working we carried his boss's I.D. to Council Bluffs and bought a bottle of Kool-aid-flavored, orange vodka. We sat on the river side of Playland Park and drank warm, Lucite-colored firewater, leaning against the back wall of the stock car track. "California," he said. "I'm gonna go to California. Land of the midnight sun. Fuck my way from San Francisco to L.A., then turn around and start back." Long sigh. "You know, if you think about it long enough, you realize that there's nothing to stop you. Nothing at all. There's you, and out there, there's what you want. The rest is just bullshit." Within a month he was gone. It was just a few weeks before his graduation. Laura's friends said that he left because he couldn't face the dances and the parties without her. Somebody suggested that he had made a deal with the school to graduate by mail; someone else said he joined the Navy. I called both his jobs. The restaurant owner and the clothier both said that he told them that he was leaving and took his pay. Laura cowered through the end of the year even though the chorus in the hall had stopped, trailing at the edges of things like an uncertain dancer hugging the shadows along the wall.

"Say you got a girl in your car, you know, and you got her blouse unbuttoned and her brassiere is loose so her tits are right out there in the open like . . ."

"Yeah."

"Say you did that, you know . . ."

"Yeah."

"Well, what would you do then?"

Jimmy the Duke, South-Side busboy, had stopped me at the door to the hotel basement. He was leaning against a steel rack of pots and pans, eager for a reply.

"Kiss 'em."

"Huh?"

"Just lean down and kiss 'em."

"You wouldn't, would you?"

"Damned right, I would."

"You're disgusting, you know that?"

"Why?"

"Damned right, he's disgustin'. Been disgustin' me for years. Sometimes I can't cook for lookin' at him." Leo scuffing by, checkered cook's pants frayed at the cuffs, trailing behind his heels.

"Said if he got a girl's brassiere off, he'd kiss her on the tits. It's enough to make you sick."

Leo turns back, stalking me with a slotted spoon. "Kiss 'em? Kiss 'em? Is that what you said?"

"He asked me, Leo, what I'd do."

"And you said 'Kiss 'em,' did you?" He was shouting and waving the spoon in my direction. "How many times I got to tell you, you *suck* 'em." Then to Jimmy—"Don't you ask Kiddo no questions about girls, hear. You got questions, you come to me." Jimmy decided to take Leo's side whatever it was and tried to smile his way out of a worsening situation. "How big were they?"

"What?"

"The tits. This big?" He cupped his free hand up to Jimmy's face and rotated an imaginary melon. "Or this big?" A cherry.

"In between."

"Like this?" A small orange or a tangerine.

"I guess."

"Well, in that case you're talkin' about titties, and Kiddo's right—you kiss titties. You don't suck 'em till they're tits." He turned and headed back to his steam table, rattling his hanging pots and pans with a triumphantly raised spoon.

"You lookin' to fight me?" Jimmy the Duke worked hard at being as tough as Frankie, the Marlon Brando imitator.

"No."

"Then you better not do that shit to me again."

"What shit?"

"You know what I mean?"

"She asked you to kiss 'em, right?"

"No.

"What she ask you to do?"

"She didn't ask me nothin'. She said, 'You been tryin' to get that off all year. Now you did, what you gonna do?' "

"Well?"

"Well what?"

"What did you do?"

"Took her home."

"Good thinkin'."

"You makin' fun a me?"

"Why don't you ask Frankie what he'd do?"

"I already did."

"What did he say?"

"He said he don't fool with brassieres." Later in the shift, when the two of us were loading dishes and clean silver off the dishstand for the coffee shop, he said, "Me neither."

"You neither what?"

"I don't fool with brassieres, not anymore."

"Don't blame you at all," said Louie, "full a hooks and wires. Tear up your pecker. Use panties like everybody else."

"You stay outa this, you old fart."

"Gotta have the ones that's been worn, though, else you might as well try your gramma's handkerchief."

Jimmy the Duke slammed the full silverware rack into the

swinging door to the dining room and went out into the safer clatter of evening diners.

"That boy's about as useless as a rubber in a maternity ward," Louie said as the door slammed shut.

In the Castle Hotel kitchen anything less than a well-acted degeneracy was dangerous. When ever anyone passed Charlie, the butcher, he'd say, "What tastes better, cunt or cabbage?" An answer was required. "I don't know, I don't eat cabbage" was a good one. "With or without carraway seeds" was even better. When Jimmy refused to play the game, Charlie told Walter and Arnie, the two gay busboys on the night shift, separately and in confidence, that he was worried about Jim because he didn't seem to have the same "interests" as the other boys. Both of them propositioned him by the end of the week. When he threatened violence, Walter retreated, but Arnie, who liked *rough stuff*, as he called it, wrestled him around a bit in the locker room. When Jimmy went to Frankie for sympathy and assistance, Frankie misunderstood the explanation and went to Arnie to negotiate a hike in Jimmy's fee. The next day Arnie was back in the locker room waiting for Jimmy the Duke with five dollars, and the fight started all over again.

If Jimmy the Duke had been at Tech High, he would have been lined up with Alvin and company along the walk sucking out kissing noises at Phil. It was an easy virtue, especially since his fears were the same as theirs. At the hotel, he missed the change in the rules of play. In the school corridor reluctance and anxiety were made virtues; they were *cool*, or at least, one version of *cool*. The only remaining collective fear in the kitchen was immobility. Nearly everyone there except Louie claimed always to be about to leave. I liked Louie for his willingness to face his own inevitabilities; washing dishes, drinking wine, and living with whores—they were what he did. He was a "dee-generate," as he said, and, so, was free of censure. Phil was a pioneer, more heroic than free, with the same burdens heros always bear. I never said so, but I admired him for his daring and his unshakable vision.

There was a rigorousness to the accepted, *cool* existence the fourth-floor chorus enforced with such brutality. The hierarchy of cars was part of it, as were the specific social registers created by fashion. Collars worn up or open or pressed flat and buttoned, lace dickies and angora tie-on collars, leather jackets, suede jackets, nylon jackets, cardigans—all had closely defined functions. Even disorder and delinquency had fashions that were carefully monitored. There were rankings for food, rituals of consumption, schedules of brand names. And sex— everyone's shimmering goal and darkest terror—had the most intricate set of rules, but it was also a bit like close-order drill on a cliff's edge. Any error could mean disaster, but there were no real prescriptions for success either, beyond simply *doing it*. A great deal of attention was given to breasts and brassieres. Opening a blouse and getting a brassiere off was a goal that was given so much attention that, in Jimmy the Duke's case anyway, achieving it left him nothing to do but start all over again on another article of clothing. Group sex—gang-banging, really, since it was a sport of groups of males and single females—was very popular. It spared the participants the terrible errors isolation could create and spared them, as well, the hideous uncertainty of nothing-to-do. The same guys who taunted Phil in the hall spent frequent Saturday nights in groups of five or six paying Dirty Mary to masturbate them in the backseat of someone's car, with oleo margarine at fifty cents a head.

The object of so much desire and elaborate strategy was tainted. Or was it tainting, with a stain deeper than disease or odor, secret and powerful? The dilemma of power is always powerlessness and defeat. The companion fear of potency stylized into a contest is castration and impotence. The dread reward of an obsession with oral subjugation is its enactment. Like the Bomb, whose power bent back on us in nightmare, sex threatened to take more than it gave. Sex was something you did to a girl, an act through which she was defeated; the fear was always that she would do something to you in the process.

Out of anger and frustration I tried often to escape it all. Dating was, I decided, a tyranny organized by the people around me, in which the school collaborated. One night, sitting on an empty hillside road through an unfinished housing development with a girl named Arlene, I tried to explain it all. "What's the point of necking," I said. "We start and stop and start again. Why don't we do something different."

"Like what?"

"Take off all our clothes, pee in the bushes together, I don't know."

"You're crazy."

"Look, this is what they want us to do. I'm supposed to try something. You're supposed to stop me. We could go on like this forever. Why don't we just start someplace else?"

"Why don't you just take me home."

Obviously, it was not possible to negotiate a change in the rules. The looney-tunes sophistication that thrived in the steam of the hotel kitchen could thrive only there. Like the model cool that swayed in perpetual motion along Twenty-fourth Street, it was bizarre, even dangerous, elsewhere.

After a cool good-night on Arlene's front porch, I drove around the city for a while to shake the frustration and give my car a chance to do its work where it performed best, alone on empty, darkened streets. In a gas station on north Sixteenth I saw Russell sitting with his feet out the door of his black Pontiac. The hood was up, and the radiator was dripping brown water into a dark stream that trailed across the pavement and ran into the street.

"Radiator core," he said instead of hello, "can't get it fixed till tomorrow."

"Come on, I'll drive you home."

He pulled a black Stetson from the seat beside him, then reached over the back of the front seat for a small, pressed-paper suitcase. After he slid both Stetson and suitcase into the

Plymouth, he walked over to the station attendant. They made an arrangement about the Pontiac, and Russell gave him his keys.

"Were you goin' somewhere or just comin' back?"

"Goin'. I was gonna spend a few days with my uncle on the reservation in Macy."

"I'll take you."

"Naw, man, you don't have to do that."

"Nothin' better to do. Can you get back?"

"Sure, Calvin's up there. I can ride back with him."

"Okay, then, let's go."

Russell protested until we passed Locust Street, where I would have turned off toward the river if I had been taking him home to East Omaha, then settled in for the ride, north on the boulevard that curves along the river bluffs, past Fort Omaha and Florence Station, where the Mormons crossed the river on their way west. At the first bend in the old Blair Road, the city flicked off behind us like an electric light. We talked about old times and drank from a bottle of Thunderbird Red Russell had rolled in a pair of pants in his suitcase. Two-lane blacktop reeled into the headlights out of the darkness ahead. The music on the radio faded a little with each dip in the road. When we pulled into the tractor road that led up to Russell's uncle's farm, the sky had lightened. There was a small frame house, almost square, lifted off the ground on four groups of concrete blocks. The farmyard was littered with loose pieces of farm equipment and the salvage of two or three cars. I pulled up beside a doorless pickup truck.

"No point in waking everybody up," Russell said, and he slid open the door to a small shed. It smelled of chickens and crankcase oil. "Take whichever bed you like." I settled into a tractor tire by the door, and Russell stretched out against a feed sack. He woke me sometime in the afternoon and asked if I wanted some breakfast or if I was going to sleep all day.

No one in the family treated my presence as anything special. The children playing in the yard barely paused as we passed. Alice, Russell's aunt, said good morning with a slightly reproachful tone, the way a mother greets a child who has overslept, and handed me a bowl of Frosted Flakes. The house was spare, one room served as kitchen and parlor-range, refrigerator and sink on one side and a brown space heater on the other. We sat at a chrome and marbled-gray vinyl dinette set on the kitchen side. The parlor was marked off by a familiar rose-patterned linoleum and had a matching couch and chair of forest green tufted nylon. There was a daybed in the corner covered with the same textured gray drapery material that was hung across the doorway to the other half of the house.

We spent the afternoon with Leroy, Russell's uncle, and Calvin, his cousin, stretching fence wire in a field some distance from the house. There seemed to be no reason for the fence. The freshly planted posts ran a short way across the middle of an uncultivated field. When I asked what it was for, Leroy laughed and said it was an "improvement." For dinner Alice gave us bowls of pinto beans in potato broth with bits of salt pork and fried bread. I talked about heading back. They all seemed disappointed, and Leroy told me that if I stayed we could all dream together. It didn't make much sense, but leaving seemed a bad idea.

Calvin had arranged a circle in the dusty yard, an old office chair with wicker frayed out at the back, the front seat from an old car, and two chairs from the dinette set. Leroy took the office chair, Russell the car seat. Calvin motioned me into one of the kitchen chairs and took the other for himself.

"There were Fire-keepers," Calvin said, "and they worked at a bunch of logs till they were dry and smooth, no more than three or four inches across and ten, maybe twelve feet long. Then they would dig a hole in the lodge, like this." He drew a semi-circle in the dust with a stick. "With the round part facing east. All day they kept a fire in this hole until it was red hot, all coals, no flames and no smoke. Then they would bring in the long poles and put the ends together over the fire." He drew four lines that touched inside the base of the semi-circle and flared slightly as they trailed back. "See, it's a bird. Then, all night long, they would keep the fire going, fanning it with feathers so it would move down the poles. When the poles burnt down, they brought in fresh ones and set them right on the ashes. It burned like that, head and tail, until the sun came up."

"You guys still do that stuff?"

"Naw. Leroy saw it once, though." Leroy's bib overalls bagged out from his bare chest. He looked up from his work boots and nodded.

On the prairie, evening hesitates briefly above the residual heat of the day, like a mirage on the highway quavering on a film of liquid air. A stand of cottonwoods in the distance darkened into cloud shapes, tipped red at their crowns. Long foxtails in the ragged field tilted on the weight of their own shadows. I watched my shadow and Calvin's lengthen in the dust. Russell dozed off on the car seat across from me, his head bobbing twice against his chest, then lolling to one side. Tree locusts in the distance began whirring out their nightsong. Leroy pulled a cloth sack from his pocket, a bank pouch marked Sioux City State Bank, untied the string at the top, and upended it, shaking a single button into his hand. He smoothed the sack across his knee and put the button in the center. With his pocket knife he cut three wedges from the circle like pieces from a small cake.

"Why just three."

"Russell's the Fire-Keeper." Calvin laughed, pointing at Russell, whose head had slipped down to the base of the seat.

I looked at the wedge Leroy put in my palm. "What now?"

"It's just like they say, man. Eat it."

It was like mud pie on my tongue, inert and repellent. I bit down, and it burst into flame, scorching the roof of my mouth. Calvin passed me a mason jar of corn liquor, and I gulped at it. He was laughing the way my grandfather laughed when I fanned the fire his banana peppers caused in my mouth. "Shit!" I sat there, elbows on my knees, my head pressed between my hands, sucking at the night air. Suddenly there was a knot in my stomach, and my throat surged and burned.

"Don't puke in the yard, man. Alice don't like it."

I stumbled into the weeds at the edge of the yard and retched. What came up had the same fire in it that corn liquor had briefly quenched in my mouth. It seared at my throat and burned its way into my nose and eyes. I could hear them laughing behind me as I knotted down over foxtails and blue stems. The spasms in my stomach continued long after it was empty. Every retch brought fresh fire. "Bastards," I said, heading back to the yard, "that stuff is rotten. It made me sick."

"It's all right, man. Sit down."

"Sit down, my ass. I think you just poisoned me."

"It's all right. Sit down."

Across the yard Leroy raised a coffee can to his face.

"I ain't gonna stay here and get poisoned."

Russell stirred from his sleep. "Poison the white eyes," he muttered. I crossed the yard to my car.

"Where you goin'?"

"To the hospital. Home. I don't know."

"Sit down, man, you can't drive now."

"Have a little more corn." Calvin waved his mason jar in my direction.

I drove south toward Decatur, my stomach and throat still burning, the Plymouth's windows wide open, both wings turned directly into my face. I was certain that I had a fever. Coming over a slight rise I noticed an odd fork in the road ahead, a second highway brightly lit that veered to the right and upward, as though following the face of a steep hill that was not there. I tried to blink it away. There was a pull toward it that seemed at first to be a fault in the car, then I realized that I was edging the car in its direction, or, rather, I felt the urge to steer toward it, since the car was still moving on flat, ordinary pavement. It was keeping its distance, waiting for my doubts to subside.

The second road was lovely, like a silver ribbon that lifted and furled, banking as it turned westward, a finely worked contrail spiraling against the pure lapis of the summer sky. It bent over the horizon, dipping and turning, brightening as it went, as though it were gathering back the rays of the vanished sun as it curled over the converging lines of distant cornfields. Quicksilver, it flowed like a shimmering stream—westward, over the long, brown spread of the plains, over the divided Platte and the ferrous neon of Chimney Rock, over the Rockies, raised like thighs. I pulled the wheel toward it and was jolted by tires thudding into a soft, rutted shoulder, weed crowns splitting across the bowsprit of the *Mayflower* at the point of the Plymouth's hood. The car came to a stop. Locusts in the fields played like blues saxophonists, and the silver road beckoned like cool water. I pulled the keys from the ignition and threw them out the right window into the field beyond. The road flicked a deep red, and the air around me tightened. Sixteen percent by volume, first demonstrated by enclosing air in a cylinder above a dish of mercury; as the mercury oxidized, the piston above the reddening metal descended. Sixteen percent. I couldn't breathe. The road softened to silver tinted a faint blue. The square-rigger on the hood dipped and plunged, spiked weed tips spilling their seeds around its bow like sea foam. Crickets laughed thick, Indian laughs all around me.

I fell asleep and dreamt of swimming in soft skin, upstream in a slow, warm current, like Missouri River shallows in late summer, thick with silt, glowing like amber, with water-grasses and nerve fibers brushing my legs. A light flared in the distance, and the skin boiled and split. I was face down in flesh, mouthing for air like a mud-beached catfish.

When I woke up, the silver road in the sky was gone. To the west there was a bare space in the cornfield, a clay circle with the burnt-out remains of the firebird Calvin had described earlier, smoking in its center. But the head was facing west, not east, and the ashen tail flared toward me. Calvin and Russell stood at the corners of the semi-circular head. They were wearing dime store versions of buckskin shirts with suede-cloth fringes and printed beadwork, looking my direction and smiling. Then they bent down to the spent firepit of the bird's head, hooked their fingers under it, and lifted it, intact, up against the blue sky, as easily as if it were a painted flat on a stage. It stood there on its tail, smoldering. Propped up, it looked more like a mushroom than a bird, made slightly mobile by the wafting of its smoke in a light breeze. The corn tassels that fringed the circle around it subsided. The cornfield fell away. As it grew larger, the ash lines of the tail merged into a single, gray stem, its crown broadening in its ascent into the darkened dome of the sky.

At sunrise, the cornfield was whole again, its sharply veined leaves and drooping tassels wet with dew. Remnant fog had gathered like rainwater in the ditch my Plymouth was sloping into. By the time I found my keys, my Levi's were soaked to the knees, and my shirt front was spotted with dew.

autoclysms

Once a year the police would send an officer around to all the high schools to talk on safe driving and show "traffic school" movies, in which a few safety tips were spliced together with footage of the most incredible gore—decapitations, split faces, severed arms and legs, chests impaled on steering columns, kneecaps sheared away by the undersides of glove compartments. The idea was to show us all as vividly as possible the consequences of careless or reckless driving. It was a horror film about cars, and in appreciation of a familiar genre the audience gasped, screamed. Some people left the auditorium holding their mouths with both hands, but the effect the program had was almost the opposite of what had been planned by the police. What was being shown was the hellfire and damnation of the automobile; like most horror movies, what we saw was a kind of oblique, exaggerated pornography. It was exhilarating, made you eager to get out to the parking lots and get going down Burt Street or up Cummings, tires screeching, to try it out, winding toward what the screen had played, always certain that at the last second it could be avoided, the denser purple where the flesh was opened and spent.

Heading home on U.S. 25, the flat river road back from the gravel pits, past Offutt Air Force Base toward South Omaha. The river casts up each summer night a thin fog that snares in the headlights. Sunburned skin tightening across my shoulders and twinged where the night air raises goose bumps on my arm. 1948 Plymouth 2-door sedan trembling at sixty on four-dollar tires. A sudden rush of high beams from behind and the fog around us snaps on like a fluorescent light. Arnie Brasher in his brother's Olds 98 convertible swings past Linda, Darlene, and Meatball, waving and screaming, kicks it into passing gear, and they flash ahead. Route 25, one of those two-lane U.S. highways with deep drainage ditches on both sides. The Olds is running flat out, way ahead, going ninety at least. Arnie swings back into the right lane just as he crosses a small bridge, the kind your tires thump over quickly, almost unnoticed, and the Oldsmobile Rocket 98 jumps up like a clown from a jack-in-the-box, skidding sideways briefly on two wheels, then nosing forward into an end-over-end front flip, chrome accessories, headlights, Arnie, Linda, Darlene, and Meatball lifted up into the fog as well, arms and legs spread wildly, swimmers just for that instant, and you recall the chill that snatched at your legs as you kicked through the quarry's skim of sunlit warm water, the terrifying cold that grappled at you all day long from the farthest corners of the cut stone below.

Five of us driving through Spirit Lake. We stop for hot dogs and A&W root beers with all four doors of the green Buick Roadmaster opened to the lake breeze. The drive-in parking lot backs into the space behind a towing company garage, and we amble over to inspect the wreckage, carrying frosted mugs and the butt ends of chili dogs. The center of attention is the corpse of a Studebaker Golden Hawk, "front-ended," somebody says—hood creased in half like a piece of paper, fenders collapsed, most of the engine driven into the front seat. The steering wheel is suspended over the dashboard by a single, twisted spoke, and the windshield is a spider's web of fractures radiating from a single point on the passenger side where forehead met safety glass: here and there bits of glass hang in marquis chips from the exposed, sticky safety center, and just below the headprint, embedded in the broken glass and rubbery film, stubbed out but intact, with the feathery print of lipstick on its white tip, an L&M filter cigarette. A few strands of blond hair caught there as well, flashing into view just where they cross out of the shadow of the roof-line into the sunlight, seem suspended in the air. The mangled front end, impacted bumper and grillwork, fenders closed like concertinas, all of it radiates from that collision in the glass, as though the whole wreckage were a crystal whose center was perfect and which grew amorphous only at its most extreme edges—a geode, then, revealing in its deadly amethyst the impeccable record of the moment of impact, down to the microsecond in which the fissures in the glass opened to receive the tip of the burning cigarette. It verges on the sublime. Verges? It's hard to imagine anything more awesome, more eloquent in its obedience to natural law, and it is impossible, slouched back in the Buick, not to imagine her beauty, the thin veil of soft perfection played out between glass and bone like the mucus you pull from the corner of your eye and press between your finger and your thumb.

In Iowa again, heading south through a flat stretch in the unremitting cornfields in a 1956 Chrysler 300, trailing a small sailboat, a Snipe. Up ahead an oncoming pickup truck stops and waits to turn left onto a farm road; a two-tone Mercury hardtop, unable to stop, starts around into our lane, sees the Ford station wagon just in front of us, and cuts back too sharply, begins to drift, heeling over toward a full roll. The Ford catches the Mercury's left taillight, sends it flying off in one piece, and the impact rights the Merc, angling it off into the ditch. The Ford careening now, but slowing fast. Not a chance of our stopping on the roadway, so we head for the ditch at an easy angle, working fine until we hit bottom and come up short against the side of the farmer's access road, the 300's big grill wedged into the culvert, jostle sharply, all of us, and fall back. Then, like punctuation, the Snipe lurches off its trailer and breaks through the Chrysler's big rear window, spraying glass like the flakes of foam that fall from the bow when it cuts through a cresting wave. The station wagon has made a try for the farm road and tips slowly over the edge on the far side, gas tank and rear axle exposed. We climb up out of our ditches, everyone, like amphibians, slithering and clumsy, and the farmer sits in his truck, unperturbed, bemused, as he might sit any raucous Saturday night leaning against the side of Atlantic, Iowa's volunteer firehouse.

It occurs to me that all of this must have gone by in just an instant for him—a sudden flurry all around him as he was turning home, from which somehow three cars and a boat angled off into various ditches like billiard balls in a trick shot. For us it had another kind of time. There is a special slowness to the accident you're in, an articulation of the segments of motion that hangs it all in an intolerable suspension. As soon as the Mercury began to slide, all the clocks changed. The slow musculature of its tilt toward us, for example, had deliberation without volition, a dance of inevitabilities, tires straining at the front edge, the sheered-off taillight bulged away from the rear fender at the station wagon's insistence like a droplet blown loose of its faucet in the wind, our descent into the ditch and the Snipe's lunge, their slow clarity. It has to do with the sudden perception of cause, I think, as well as with increased adrenaline and focused attention, an instantaneous etiology that alters the perception of time.

In Omaha, the last day of the 1948 Plymouth, driving down the easy hill past St. Joseph's Hospital, where I was born, circumcised, had my tonsils out, and my arms and nose pieced back together after my great bicycle accident, passing the nurses' dorms on the right, nearing the far edge of the grounds, with my friend David in the front seat and David's mother and his brother, Kenny, in back. A fish truck pulls away from the stop sign on the left. I honk, skid to a stop, and the fish truck slogs on, slowly pushing its big, welded iron breastwork into the Plymouth's side. We wait for it to stop—the crunching of metal and glass, the slow grind of the grill cover toward my face, the whine of the truck's low gear. It goes on. The Plymouth lifts slightly, the truck dozing us sideways out of the intersection. The door is almost against the steering wheel. The horn still sounds, and I am seated like a passenger in the middle of the front seat. It stops, the Plymouth settling back, the fish truck's mouth heaving away.

We all climb out of the car stiffly like sleepers waking in a draft. The fish truck driver, who obviously froze with his foot on the truck's gas pedal, comes out of it screaming about speeders and reckless teenage drivers. My car is bent in the middle, and David's mother has torn her dress. An intern looks into my eyes briefly, then stares at my head, reaches up, and picks a long sliver of glass from my hair and places it carefully in my hand, then returns to my head with both hands, like a chimpanzee grooming for lice, until my hand is full of various bits of glass. The fishmonger wants me off the street. A policeman writes everything down and quietly arrests him. A fish company representative, out of nowhere, asks if anyone was badly hurt, assures me that I'll be taken care of and promises David's mother a new dress. Spectators, mostly disappointed at the lack of serious injury, trail off. It was a dull accident, an execution, really.

A Saturday, all morning spent making No. 2 pencil marks inside parallel blue dots on the College Board Exam answer sheet. At the lunch break we all drive off in a freezing rain to a drive-in for hamburgers and french fries. Afterward we drive around on the glassine streets, four cars eventually out on the parkway along Happy Hollow, happily sliding long glissades under the iced-over elm trees. Lovely, how the wheel spins so freely in your hands and the long delay the car takes responding, finally tacking into another long, curling sway. We are going around a second time, moving toward the curb. I touch the brake, and the car seems to speed up, turn the wheel and the rear end fish-tails slightly, the curb coming on quickly now, surprising how it jolts you back to earth, the steering wheel whipped round on impact. It softens again as we slide along the iced grass and nudge still against a tree, shaking ice down on us in a great clatter. We push the car back on the road, my green Oldsmobile with the great chrome scowl, drive carefully back to an afternoon of math and science, those green pencils and blue printed booklets on long cafeteria tables—one stroke up and one stroke down between the faint blue curb-lines under A, B, C, or D, the jerky guesswork you make a future out of, obliterating that other icy-smooth quickness and the graceful catastrophes it played at for an hour after lunch, for two or three years, in fact, at various speeds, on asphalt, concrete, gravel, and clay, as well as ice, so many dead or damaged, the almost endless stretch of shattered glass and bent metal, bodies bent and broken, Meatball hung like loose newspaper against a barbed-wire fence, Linda facedown in the sumpwater in the ditch, Darlene's unmarked body at the edge of a cornfield, her head severed by a telephone pole guide wire found in a furrow at first light, the girl in the Golden Hawk kissing her breath away on that memorial cigarette.

My friend David told me that after the accident in the Plymouth I drove far less cautiously. There is something irresistible about crashing and a certain invulnerability that goes with having just once totaled a car. Even the slang gave it a special authority: "Anania totaled his car!" Among all those active verbs—chopped, channeled, nosed, decked, peeled, creamed—that one held sway. *Totalled.*

"You hear what happened to Arnie?"

"Hear? Man, he's just passed us on the road when it happened."

"No shit?"

"No shit! You could see 'em flying off in every direction."

"What hit him?"

"Nothin', just went over that crick bridge a little bit crooked goin' 90-95 and did a full front roll. You could see 'em all, all four of 'em, fly off to the sides a the road."

"Musta totaled the Olds, eh?"

"Arms and legs out, towels, bathing suits, everything in the car . . ."

"They all dead?"

"Guess so. They all looked dead. Darlene's head was gone, man, just gone, and Meatball, he was covered all over with blood."

"Musta totaled that 98, I guess."

"Totaled? Yeah, if that's what you say when a car's spread out halfway to Bellevue."

"You see Darlene's head?"

"Naw, they were still lookin' for it when we left."

michael anania

was born in Omaha, Nebraska in 1939. He attended the University of Nebraska, the University of Omaha, and the State University of New York at Buffalo. He has published *The Color of Dust* and *Riversongs*, both collections of poetry, and numerous critical articles on contemporary poetry and on small press publishing. He currently lives in Chicago with his wife and teenage daughter, and he is on the faculty of the University of Illinois-Chicago.

other books by
michael anania:

The Color of Dust *1970*
Set/Sorts *1974*
Riversongs *1974*
New Poetry Anthology *1969*

other fine titles from
      Thunder's Mouth Press